"I have a couple of conditions...

"Rehire the groundskeeper and you take on the operations director role for the summer. You know what the old owner used to do."

Walker held Trisha's gaze for a moment, then nodded. "Done." His quick decision to trust her warmed her heart.

"You may find you can continue to do some tasks once you start your tech job back up," she said. "That way we could look for someone more qualified to be the barn manager and do a few operations director tasks."

"So you'll do it?"

She gazed into his mesmerizing eyes and shook away the distraction he caused her. It might not be easy, but she'd do it for the children. "Sure."

She lifted her chin.

Somehow they'd have to find a way to work the farm and care for the children.

Somehow they'd have to succeed.

A soft nicker in the distance drew her attention to the quaint barn filled with well-loved horses. Could she successfully manage the barn and not become entrapped in Walker's snare?

Heidi Main writes sweet inspirational romance novels set in small towns. Though she lives in central North Carolina's suburbs, she dreams of acreage and horseback riding, which is why her novels include wide-open ranches and horses. Before starting her writing career, Heidi worked with computers and taught Jazzercise. A perfect Saturday is lounging on the deck with her husband and watching the many birds in their backyard. Learn more about her books at heidimain.com.

Books by Heidi Main

Love Inspired

A Nanny for the Rancher's Twins
A Family for the Orphans

Visit the Author Profile page at LoveInspired.com.

A Family
for the Orphans

Heidi Main

LOVE INSPIRED
INSPIRATIONAL ROMANCE

LOVE INSPIRED®

INSPIRATIONAL ROMANCE

Recycling programs for this product may not exist in your area.

ISBN-13: 978-1-335-59706-9

A Family for the Orphans

For questions and comments about the quality of this book, please contact us at CustomerService@Harlequin.com.

Love Inspired
22 Adelaide St. West, 41st Floor
Toronto, Ontario M5H 4E3, Canada
www.LoveInspired.com

Printed in U.S.A.

For we walk by faith, not by sight.
—*2 Corinthians* 5:7

To God be the glory.

Acknowledgments

Rich and Ashlyn, thank you for believing in me and the constant encouragement while I chase this writing dream of mine.

Mindy Obenhaus, for listening to my story ideas and helping me tweak them just so. I couldn't have done this without you and greatly appreciate all of your help.

Shado Alvarado, since I live in suburbia, you are my go-to for farm and ranch information. Thank you for your friendship and enduring countless animal questions these past years.

Jodie Bailey, girl we did it! You had faith in me and my writing when I had none. Thanks for the coffee meetings and all the encouragement you have given me over the years.

Chapter One

Trepidation over the coming months clawed Trisha Campbell's gut as she gripped the smooth metal handle and pushed open the farmhouse door. She grinned at what sounded like a herd of stampeding elephants coming from above. Walker and the kids must have heard her arrival and scrambled to the top of the stairwell. She was excited about seeing Sophie, Tommy and Gabby again, but her smile dimmed at the sorrowful reason she was here—the sweet children had suddenly become orphans.

Four months ago, Walker McCaw was named guardian to Parker and Avery's three young children after the horrific helicopter accident. Trisha, an Iowa State University professor, had been named backup guardian. She hadn't felt the least bit competent to ease their pain since her role models had been lousy. Especially after Sophie's freak-out on her first-grade graduation day, Tommy pretending like nothing had changed, and Gabby's constant teary-eyed missing her mommy and daddy.

Trisha closed the front door behind her, trapping the humid Texas air outside; she hoped moving to the country and living in a different home would help the children.

As the kids hurried down the steps, Trisha rolled her tight shoulders, exhausted from her overnight twelve-hour drive from Iowa. She had an entire summer to help the children heal and assist Walker with this newly purchased horse farm, yet somehow it all sounded overwhelming.

The excited kids burst off the bottom step. Sophie reached her first, clinging tight. "I missed you." The seven-year-old's whisper brought quick tears to Trisha. She blinked them back. She had to stay strong for the kids, but the undercurrent of those three words wrapped around her heart and brought back memories of losing her mother years ago as a young child, making her feel helpless and unloved. Right now, the desperation in Sophie's hug gave her more determination to help the sweet orphans as much as possible during these coming eight weeks, so they'd understand they could rely on her.

As Walker lumbered down the last of the carpeted steps, she eyed the sudden single dad to three young children. Between Sophie's school year ending, packing up and moving here from their cottage in downtown Serenity and understanding the semantics of running a horse farm, she understood the dark smudges under his eyes. She only hoped she could be of some help to him as well.

Sophie sniffed and clutched tighter. Then Tommy squeezed in. "What about me? Sheesh." The five-year-old wrapped his arms around Trisha's middle. She leaned down and kissed the top of his head, his curls tickling her nose. How could this little one be about to enter kindergarten? It devastated her that Avery wouldn't be here to pick out his outfit, give him a reassuring hug or take his picture stepping onto the bus. A lump clogged in Trisha's throat and refused to budge. Why had God taken Parker and Avery and left these children orphaned?

"Me, me," Gabby insisted as the little three-year-old jockeyed for position.

Trisha leaned down and lifted Gabby, breathing in her sweet-smelling baby shampoo. Gabby held on as if she hadn't been hugged in forever, but that wasn't true. She clung to Walker all the time—it seemed Gabby was always stuck on his hip when they'd video chatted. Trisha swiped away a tear before it rolled down her cheek. Over the past eight years, she had visited her friends and their children in Serenity, Texas, countless times. They'd become like a second family to her. She had even slipped into holidays and vacations as though she belonged with them, but she really hadn't. Now she hoped the special times she'd shared with the children would benefit them.

"Are you really going to teach us to trot and canter, take us on trail rides and, you know, play with us?" Sophie asked.

"Of course, sweetie. I'm all yours for eight weeks." Walker had so much on his plate, their plan was for Trisha to focus on the kids. She set a squirming Gabby on the ground.

Walker shifted and caught her eye. College life, and then his career in the computer field, had molded him into a clean-shaven, business-attire-wearing professional. But today he looked the part of a cowboy, sporting faded blue jeans, a solid blue chambray shirt, and clutching a worn Stetson, exactly how she remembered him from the summer he'd worked alongside her at his family's cattle ranch. The scruff on his face made him appear tired and the top of his brown hair was matted, showing the outline of his cowboy hat.

"We were just straightening a few things upstairs." His low Texas drawl rumbled through the space as he tilted his head to the stairwell.

"Did you bring it?" Sophie's rushed words ran together.

Trisha ripped her gaze from Walker's, dug into her purse and lifted the requested label maker. Sophie's eyes lit up as she took it.

The girl waved the item at her. "There are tons of shelves in our bedroom closet—you've gotta see it. It's ginormous. I'm going to label all the shelves to organize my folded clothes." Her wide smile disappeared. "My mommy was the best at folding."

Trisha engulfed the girl in a hug. "If you like, I'd love to help organize your closet." The excitement lining the girl's eyes gave Trisha hope that she'd be able to acclimate the children to their new house and property, and that it would soon feel like home for them.

"How about I help you this afternoon, Sophie, right before dinner?"

The girl nodded, her chin wavering. Trisha gave her another squeeze while the other kids clamored for her attention.

"You gotta see Treasure, the pony Walka got us." Tommy rolled his eyes and tipped his head to his sisters. "They named him."

Sophie and Gabby bounced on their toes. "Please?"

It warmed Trisha's heart to see the children so happy. "Absolutely. Lead the way." The kids clamored out the door and down the porch steps.

Now that they were alone, she speared Walker with a look. "How are they doing?" Four months since their parents' deaths. Four months with Walker as their guardian and Trisha as the backup. Four months of almost daily phone calls as Walker had done his best to help the children navigate their loss while Trisha doled out encouragement and advice, best as she could. But what did either of them know about parenting?

He held her gaze for a drawn-out moment and something passed between them, just like in February when she'd come for the memorial service. She shook it off because she had zero interest in a relationship with him or anyone. Not after her past mistakes.

"Not bad. The horse farm has given them something else to focus on." He ran a palm over his handsome face, releasing an appealing scent of his aftershave. "They each remember the day they toured Serenity Stables with their parents and talked about living here. I think that helps them."

They stepped out of the house and crossed the gravel lot, trailing after the kids. Walker stuck his cowboy hat on and waved at a mom with two teenagers walking from their dusty minivan to the upper barn. Likely the teens boarded their horses there.

The loamy smell of dirt clung to the moist air. More than a few broken fences caught her eye, scattered new boards with weeds growing around them looked forlorn, and fields with knee-high grass screamed *mow me*. She halted. "Why isn't the groundskeeper doing his job?"

The place had been in tip-top condition when they'd viewed it in February. She had come for the memorial service and had stayed two weeks since other professors had graciously covered her classes. The kids had needed her and it was essential she and Walker come up with a plan of attack for the pending sale on this property. They had moved forward with the purchase, because that was what Parker and Avery would have wanted.

Now the obvious neglect left her distressed.

"I've been meaning to mow," Walker said. He pulled his hat off and ran his free hand through his tousled hair. Worry lines that hadn't been there before creased his forehead. "But I'm being pulled in a million different directions."

"Mowing is a task for the groundskeeper, Walker."

"The goal of the stable is to become self-sufficient, so I let Archie go." He rubbed his temples as though his head was pounding. "It's the only way we can keep it so the children can grow up here. I figure I'll mow and fix fence boards on my own. Once the kids are all moved in, I'll have more time."

"The groundskeeper did way more than that, Walker. I spoke with the previous owners when we toured the property. Archie mowed and fixed fence boards, yes, but he also handled the upkeep on the buildings, including the house and garage. He serviced the tractors and lawn mowers, cleared the trails, and probably lots of other little things that take time, which is something you won't have come September when you return to your cyber-security position."

He looked around. "Other than a little mowing and some fence upkeep, it looks fine for now. We needed to cut some of the fat. Did you know he was a salaried employee?"

She fought to keep her rising irritation at his decision under control. "But this place was running in the black when we bought it. Remember how we planned to keep as many employees as possible and backfill the vacated positions?"

"Barely in the black," he clarified. "I needed to cut costs from the start so that our long-term plan would work. Remember, I'm the numbers guy. You're the horse whisperer."

"But—"

He held up his hand like a traffic cop and his gaze sharpened. "Listen, Trisha. I'm doing the best I can. My prior life came to a screeching halt when Parker and Avery died, and I still feel like I have no idea how I'm going to raise three kids. So forgive me if I'm not always thinking clearly." His voice pierced the thick air between them like a knife. "Since the plan was to run the horse farm in the black, I had to cut the grounds-keeper to conform with our plan." He spit out *plan* as if it were a bad word.

She sucked in a breath. She'd been so worried about the kids and herself that she had given little thought to how Walker's life had changed. He'd also lost his best friends. But in addition, he had put his career on hold, sold his home to move in with the children, and now she expected him to work on a horse farm when he'd clearly chosen the computer field over his family tradition of cattle ranching.

Sophie raced the few feet back to drag Trisha to the mouth of the lower barn, a wide smile splayed on her lips. "See our barn? Not all these horses are ours, but aren't they pretty?"

"They sure are." She looked at Walker, his frown and worry creases disappearing for a moment. The kids were happy here, exactly where their parents had dreamed of raising their children.

In the lower barn, the kids each took a carrot from the basket outside Roy's vacant office. Walker McCaw ran his fingers through the itchy scruff on his chin, feeling much older than thirty lately. He lifted a hand in greeting to Ryder and Buck, the stable hands who knew everything. Right now they were at the end of the corridor, turning out the lesson horses.

"Did the kids harvest those from your mother's garden?" Trisha asked, tilting her head. He could barely see the spray of freckles dotting her creamy white nose and cheeks.

He nodded. "My mom watched the kids yesterday. She said they loved pulling the vegetables right out of the earth." Dirt clung to the carrots whose green tops now drooped against the wicker basket—wilting much like his daily energy. A sudden single dad to a three-, five- and seven-year-old? Most days, he didn't believe he could raise three kids and wondered if their lives would ever find a new normal. "My mom has an abundant supply this year, and we're more than happy to take some off her hands."

Trisha smiled. Maybe he shouldn't have snapped at her earlier, but he had a lot on his plate and, frankly, hadn't been aware of the extensive groundskeeper tasks. But Archie was gone now.

Since Walker was here, and she'd been in Iowa, she didn't have the right to second-guess his decisions. As phone buddies, they had a good relationship, but maybe being in person for the entire summer hadn't been the smartest idea.

"They seem like they're adjusting well." Her attention was on the children fast-walking down the aisle. Trisha wore Bermuda shorts, a frilly top and little sneakers—simple and classic.

"You're definitely doing a great job with them," she continued. "Your parents should be proud of you." Her voice held a wistful tone and Walker wondered again about her own family, or lack thereof.

"I hope so."

She shifted and her fresh smell, with a slight hint of citrus, wafted over. Trisha was the opposite of a girlie girl and never wore fragrances. That was one thing he liked about her.

As she stood beside him, he realized they were going to need to work more like a team. Even though Trisha was only the backup guardian, he'd called on her for parenting-type advice countless times in the past four months, which was what Parker and Avery had hoped. Especially with the decision to move forward in purchasing this place.

The children each stopped at a different stall to offer their carrot and pet a horse. The horses nickered and neighed to get their attention.

"You've trained them well. No running or quick moves around the horses." Trisha bumped his shoulder. "Good job."

At their giggles and grins, Walker let his shoulders relax. Their parents had died right in the middle of acquiring this horse farm, the children's inheritance. Though Walker had hesitated to follow through with the purchase, Trisha had encouraged it. Since the deal had closed two weeks ago, her arrival on the farm was perfect timing.

Except, Serenity Stables wasn't as successful as they'd thought, which put a crimp in their plan of making the stables profitable so the children could live there. Worse, a housing developer had called and made an aggressive bid on the horse farm land. A shiver of unease had slid down

Walker's spine at the confidence in the developer's voice when he had insisted Walker call when he was ready to sell.

"I'm glad you're here." He'd have to tell her the specifics about the books and the pushy housing developer, but not with the kids around.

"I wish I had just stayed in February and taken the semester off." She pushed a wayward strand from her face. "Sorry I didn't."

Trisha was the fixer, always had been. He was the idealist. Together, they would probably make a great team. Except, he'd been on his own for a while now, and sharing responsibility or asking for help didn't come naturally.

"You're here now." He'd never been so grateful for the teaching profession. Having her here for eight straight weeks would be a game changer for the children. And that she'd gone to college for ranch management might help them get the stable back on track.

The kids giggled when the horses took the last of the carrots and tickled their palms.

"They seem happy." Her emerald eyes twinkled and pulled him in, but he dragged his gaze away. Ever since the helicopter crash, he'd been having weird feelings toward Trisha. Except he didn't have the right to be attracted to another woman. Not after what had happened to Phoebe.

He couldn't risk another relationship where he could fail so horribly again. His focus needed to be on the success of the stable, not Trisha and her enticing everything.

Gabby scurried over to her older sister and stood on her tiptoes to pet the mare's nose.

"Where's Roy?" Trisha asked.

He craned his neck to view the front pasture and noted

small puffy clouds dotted the otherwise blue sky. Where was the barn manager? Come to think of it, Walker hadn't seen him all day.

"Around here somewhere." The man was the glue that held the stable together. Walker didn't even want to consider the hard place he'd be in if he hadn't had Roy to lean on. It'd be like handing the property over to the housing developer, and Walker refused to allow that.

At least Walker had done something right by leaning heavily on his most important employee.

"You know how key the barn manager is to this operation. We are fortunate Roy didn't follow the owners."

Trisha lifted her chin. "Yes, I thought it odd he stayed on, yet they took the horse trainer with them." Was she saying Roy wasn't a good fit for barn manager?

"The horse trainer position was redundant." He palmed his Stetson and raked his fingers through his hair. "Roy's pretty solid. He seems fine with doing both."

Her brow furrowed in confusion. "You actually asked him to do both roles? Without a pay increase?"

He wasn't sure why she didn't understand the redundancies of the roles. She'd worked at several horse farms before, so out of everyone, she should understand. This farm wasn't that big. Roy could handle it. His family's cattle ranch, the Triple C, was way bigger than this place, with fewer employees, and it was doing fine.

Sophie and Gabby, holding hands like best friends, rushed over. "Can we show Tish our pony now, please?" Sophie's pleading face looked so much like Avery's that he almost broke down. He couldn't believe she'd have to grow up motherless and traverse the rest of her life without her parents.

Well, all three children were orphans, and as expected,

they'd taken it hard for a while. The first week after they'd learned their parents weren't coming home, Tommy had cried because he couldn't find his favorite athletic shorts, Sophie had argued they shouldn't return to school, and Gabby had just wanted her mommy nonstop.

It had been a rough four months for them. But since moving to Serenity Stables, it felt like they'd come out the other side. As though moving here had allowed the children to start fresh.

He swallowed against his tight throat. "Of course you can show Tish your pony, sweetie." He tried for a smile, but it likely fell flat. Could he really parent three children? He glanced at Trisha, who was pulling her hair into a low ponytail and fastening an elastic band around it. He'd need every bit of help she was willing to give to raise them.

Sophie reached for his hand and the four of them walked down the wide aisle to the last stall, where Tommy waited for them, foot tapping.

While Walker remained in the aisle, Trisha oohed and aahed over their pony, just like the children had hoped. The docile creature let their hands touch and grab him, and he never moved. The pony might have given Walker a side-eye to complain, but maybe he was just reading into things. Walker slid his hat back on his head.

Gabby rushed over and launched herself at him. He snagged her, lifting her body to spin her around. Her excited squeal wound its way into his heart. He popped the three-year-old on his hip and she rested her head on his shoulder.

"Walka." That one sweet word formed an emotional lump in his throat that refused to budge. These kids were everything to him. "I wuv our pony." Her sweet lisp wove into his core. These kids loved it here. Somehow, he had to make this horse farm a success.

Motion caught his attention. Roy was stomping down the steps from his garage apartment, struggling to carry multiple black garbage bags tied with yellow plastic. From the hard set of the barn manager's face and his sharp movements, something was wrong.

Walker put Gabby down and caught up with the man as he hefted the bulging bags into the bed of his rusted truck. As usual, a unique body odor wafted off the man. "Everything okay?" Walker asked. He felt Trisha's presence beside him.

Roy swiveled around, his eyes shooting daggers. "I just read your email. I'm a barn manager, not a horse trainer." He finger-quoted the title. "Ya know, I can make more at a fast-food joint than what you pay me. I quit." Roy slid into the driver's seat and took off, sending gravel dust into the air.

As his truck turned into a tiny dot in the distance, Walker's shoulders slumped in defeat. He peeked at Trisha's surprised face, thankful the children were still fawning over Treasure and weren't there to see Roy leave. "I didn't think he'd mind taking on a little more responsibility."

She wrinkled her nose. "A little? Walker, the trainer role would add about twenty hours to an already full schedule," she said, then waved her hand at him. "You know, this may be for the best. I think we can find someone better than Roy."

Worry churned his gut. He was a cybersecurity geek. His specialty was discovering weaknesses in computer firewalls, not running a horse stable and keeping it afloat— that was Trisha's specialty. Though, since most of the year she lived twelve hours away, the responsibility of oversee-ing this place would fall on him.

A line of cars pulled in, the afternoon's group lesson riders. They parked and doors slammed shut. The kids and moms greeted one another and then headed to the lower barn.

Yes, he'd grown up on a cattle ranch, but that was a completely different beast. He wasn't sure how much of the business end he'd understood before he'd left for col-lege and walked away from ranching.

The kids rushed over.

"Can we ride Treasure, Walka, please?" Sophie held her hands in a praying position. "I want to show Tish how brave I am." How could Walker say no to that?

"Of course. Let's get her saddled up."

How would they care for the horses every day with-out a barn manager? The stable hands were good folk, but they needed direction.

Walker scrubbed a hand over his face. He had to fix this problem, otherwise he might not have a choice but to sell to the developer, and he absolutely would not do that.

The children could not lose this farm, the very place Parker and Avery had wanted their children raised.

Chapter Two

Walker halted on the heavily used path between the barns. Dip Dip and Lilly Bug raced over with quick high-pitched yips and jumped at his knees. While he crouched low to pet the excited Jack Russell terriers, the early morning sun warmed his back.

For three days, Walker had been attempting to do Roy's job, as well as that of the prior owners, who'd run the entire operation, and he'd been failing miserably. How had the former owners been profitable, or at least broken even?

"How are you young ladies this morning?" he asked the dogs. In response, they started tussling, growling and grabbing at each other's necks.

He stood, concerned about what looked like aggressive behavior, even though Trisha kept telling him the dogs were only playing. At the Triple C, they had calm retrievers, collies and shepherds that blended in with the background. But these little Jacks play-fought a lot and he worried the children might get caught up in one of the "friendly" tussles.

"Enough," he said with a stern voice. The dogs scrambled free and ran toward the unoccupied riding ring. Clouds of dirt lifted behind their racing paws.

Across the way, Wilbur, the dogs' owner, waved. Walker lifted a hand in response.

He still couldn't believe they had a stranger living on the property. Apparently, years ago when a family sold the farm, one of the older relatives hadn't wanted to move to Arizona with them, so they'd set him up with a life estate. Trisha thought the idea was sweet, almost like having an extra grandfather for the children, except years in cybersecurity made Walker question if this man might be a threat. Though, frankly, Walker had too many other issues to deal with than Wilbur. Four Jack Russell terriers lived with the older man and apparently had free rein on the farm. Wilbur's home was tucked into the corner of the property and they rarely saw him, but the dogs were always around.

Walker drew in the earthy smell of dirt, made a notation to order more grain, slid his phone in his pocket and then hurried to the office. As he stepped into the barn, low whinnies welcomed him, as though the horses hoped it was feeding time. Again. He rolled his eyes at the large animals he'd come to care for in such a short amount of time.

Car tires crunching over the gravel parking area drew his attention to a white minivan pulling in.

His gaze dropped to the overgrown grass near the house. If he had a half hour, he could jump on the riding mower and cut the grass. Maybe after lunch?

The mother of two young girls who boarded their Thoroughbreds popped out of the minivan and approached the barn.

"Walker McCaw?" Her jaw was rigid, as though upset.

He tipped his Stetson in greeting. "Mrs. Hudson, right?" Her heavy perfume overwhelmed him, but he didn't react because he needed every boarder they had, and this woman had two.

Her cheeks pinkened and she pushed back her perfectly coiffed hair, then tossed him a quick smile. "Yes." She cleared her throat. "I wanted to give our notice. We'll be pulling Bella and Arielle's horses at the end of June."

His shoulders slumped. "May I ask why?"

"If you must know, our loyalty lies with Roy, and he's moved to a stable not too far away." Her voice drifted off, and in that moment, Walker questioned how many boarders would leave to follow Roy. Boy, had he been wrong to ask more of the man and ultimately push him away.

Walker ran a palm over his scratchy chin. What were they going to do? He'd been hoping to increase the boarders, not lose them.

She cleared her throat again. "I'll have the transport people coordinate their travel arrangements. Good luck with Serenity Stables. Our girls will miss it." With that, she turned and left the barn.

As she got into her minivan and drove off, he stared. Why was God allowing these bad things to happen to prevent the success of the stable? He shook his head. Maybe the more important question was, why had God allowed Parker and Avery Bolden to perish in that helicopter crash? Hadn't He known how much they still needed the couple here?

Even after four busy months, an empty ache still clung to his middle because Walker missed them so much.

"We're out of hay." Buck came alongside him. "Want me to grab some?" he asked over the impatient hooves kicking their stall walls in the hope of more food or attention.

"Sure."

"How many bales?" Sweat glistened on the stable hand's forehead.

Walker had absolutely no idea. Nor did he know where it was stored. He was failing miserably. "I'll leave that up to you."

Buck tossed him a quizzical look before turning to get the hay.

If Walker failed to keep the farm afloat, the children wouldn't be able to live here like their parents had wanted. Like they themselves had wanted once they'd moved in and caught a taste of country life.

But who could take over the barn manager role and succeed?

Trisha's image floated into his mind. Yes! Why hadn't he thought of her before? She was an expert in this area. After getting her degree in horse ranch management, she'd gone into academia instead of taking a role as barn manager at an elite stable.

Excitement rose within as he realized he might have solved their problem.

He strode across the gravel lot to the house, but halfway there, his steps faltered. Could he really ask Trisha for help? She'd decided to spend her summer here so she could settle the kids on the farm while he got the place up and running, except he'd been doing a horrible job. Moving cattle from pasture to pasture differed completely from the customer-service element of boarding horses and keeping everyone happy, as Mrs. Hudson had just proved.

Would Trisha be willing to change her summer plans?

He hoped so, because she might be his last chance at making this place a success. If they didn't succeed, then Silver Developers might win.

Laughter and squeals lifted from the backyard, so he skirted the house. The sky was dark and foreboding, kind of like his day.

In the yard, Trisha was pushing Gabby in a swing, Tommy rode a dirt bike through the grass and Sophie perched on the top of the slide, hugging her knees with her face close to Trisha's, as though they were in a deep conversation.

He stopped to take in the scene. Yes, Trisha was good for the kids. Especially Sophie, the oldest, who was taking the loss of her parents harder than the other two. The children, the girls especially, needed a solid mother figure, and so far, Trisha had filled that spot for them.

It was too bad Trisha lived in Iowa. Maybe this summer would make her reevaluate and return to Texas, because the kids would love that.

Trisha glanced over and gave him a welcoming smile. She'd become a good friend these past couple of months. Maybe too good? He nudged the brim of his cowboy hat, tilting it up ever so slightly as his eyes met hers.

Gabby uttered a high-pitched squeal when she saw him. "Walka." She skidded her feet on the dirt beneath the swing to stop her motion and ran over to him. "Up, up," she stated as she reached her arms to him.

He picked her up and plopped her on his hip. "How's my big girl today?" He'd left the house before dawn while the children were still asleep, thankful Trisha had come over from the garage apartment to keep an ear out for the children while he started on the farm chores.

Gabby's sweet response was to snuggle her head into

his chest, right above his heart. The reaction about melted him into a puddle.

The kids were having such an enjoyable afternoon, now might not be the best time to talk about ranch issues. He didn't want the kids overhearing and becoming worried.

Gabby took his face in her tiny hands. "Can we have ice cweam for dessert tonight?"

He glanced at Trisha for an explanation. His eyes caught on hers and he felt a jolt to the soles of his feet. He looked away. What was going on? There was no way he had romantic feelings toward Trisha.

"Earlier, when I was getting chicken from the deep freezer, she saw a couple of gallons of ice cream. I told them they'd have to ask you. I wasn't sure what your sugar rules were."

He chuckled. Rules on sugar? He was doing anything and everything to stay afloat. If the kids wanted something, they got it. He'd found taking the least confrontational route was the easiest, and right now, the easiest sounded good. "Yes, sweetie, we can have ice cream."

Gabby lifted her arms in success, then wiggled to get down.

He turned to Trisha, but she had settled on a swing near Sophie and they appeared deep in conversation. She was so good for these kids. Him too. Before she'd arrived, he'd felt disorganized and not focused at all. With her here, he felt more grounded.

He was so thankful for her because she'd walked right into their lives and started cleaning up all the messes. She made them unite like a family and worked hard to create memories of the five of them so the children could one day move on with their lives.

With her back to him, he couldn't see her piercing green eyes, cute freckles or infectious smile. But he could see strands of auburn hair had fallen from her messy bun, highlighting her curved and feminine neck.

He tugged at the brim of his hat and focused on Tommy and his dirt bike, a wide smile on the five-year-old's face. Usually the boy rode his bike to work through feelings about his parents, but today was the first time he beamed while riding. Maybe he was getting over the worst of the grief?

His chest squeezed at the joy the kids were having. These children were his heart. No, this was not the time to have a serious conversation with Trisha.

The chat with Trisha about the barn manager's position would have to wait until the kids were in bed. He hoped she'd be amenable to it, because if she wasn't, he didn't know what to do.

Sophie looked up from her spot in front of the large coffee table strewn with small dolls, her hand gripping the waist of a Polly Pocket. "Do ya hafta go back to Iowa?" Even though Trisha had only been here four days, the girl asked daily. How come one guardian wasn't enough?

Except, deep inside, Trisha knew the answer. When she'd lost her mother, she hadn't even had an attentive father, like the children had with their guardian Walker. Since Avery and Parker had been amazing parental examples, of course the kids wanted a father figure *and* a mother figure.

Trisha crossed the living room and knelt in front of the girl. "Sweetheart, you can always video chat or call me. Anytime."

Sophie threw her arms around Trisha. "I'm so glad

you're here," she whispered. "I wish you could be here all the time." Her shoulders shook as soft sobs overtook her. Trisha's heart hiccuped at the child's confidence in her.

The little girl's eyes filled with tears and her chin trembled. "Walka just doesn't get me. He's a boy." When Sophie's jaw quivered, Trisha's heart cracked a little more.

Trisha squeezed her arms tighter, the girl's berry shampoo filling her nose. "Oh, sweetie, you have Memaw and Aunt Autumn." Walker's mother and sister had stepped up in a big way since the parents' deaths. They were better choices for Sophie.

Did the girl not see how incapable Trisha was?

Trisha didn't feel adequate for stepping into a motherly role for the children. A friend, sure. Someone to console them, absolutely. A confidante who understood losing her mother at a young age, Trisha was there for them. But since her mother had been sick, and not very maternal for years before she'd passed, Trisha was the last person qualified to step into a parental role with these children.

Sophie released her and swiped at her damp face. "Maybe you can help me get some new clothes? Mommy would call most of my clothes ratty."

Now, shopping was something Trisha could get behind. That was a friend thing, anyway. She took in Sophie's outfit. The top that used to tuck in during her last week of first grade now sat above the waist and her shorts were snug. "Of course I'll take you shopping."

How had she not noticed the ill-fitting clothing while she had helped the children unpack and organize their rooms this week? Maybe she'd been too focused on organizing Gabby's fourth birthday party.

"Wanna play?" Sophie handed her a doll, told her the role to play and focused on her toys as though the mountain of problems she'd just expressed weren't there. A shy smile crossed the girl's lips and something inside Trisha's chest clenched.

Maybe Walker would find someone and remarry. Then the children would have a new mother, or at least a mother figure.

But the hope that he'd remarry didn't comfort Trisha one bit. In fact, something that felt like jealousy overwhelmed her, and she didn't know why. She had no plans to have another relationship with anyone, so why did she care about Walker's romantic status?

Later that night, after putting the girls to bed, she pushed open the screen door to join Walker on the porch for what had turned into their daily recap. A time of day she had begun to crave yet refused to wonder why. The door clacked shut behind her and she settled on the rocker, her muscles relaxing into the soft wood. She gazed at the colorful mix of pink and blue in the sky as the sun began to set.

"Thanks for alternating putting the girls and Tommy down for the night. The kids like it and I sure appreciate the help." The clean air mixed with the tempting scent of his aftershave.

"My pleasure." She treasured her time with each of the children. She had loved them before Parker and Avery had passed away, but these past few days, their little personalities had wormed their way deeper into her heart. Leaving in a couple of months was going to be much harder than she'd imagined. She pushed off and the rocker went into motion.

Her mind flitted to the few moments earlier in the

day with Walker's mother. What an amazing woman of faith. Could Trisha find that kind of spiritual peace in Texas? After all, God had been an important part of her world before her engagement had ended and her life came crashing down around her. She hadn't realized until today that she'd been relying on herself more than God these last few years. When she and Cora had been talking, Trisha realized if she were now a role model to these three children, she'd better get back to relying on God again.

She took in Walker's masculine form and strong jawline, thinking back to how happy the kids had been since she'd arrived. At peace. She stilled, then smiled.

"You've become a good father, Walker."

"Thanks," he said. Then he put his elbows on his thighs and leaned forward in his rocker beside hers, expression worried. "Mrs. Hudson came to see me today. She's pulling Bella and Arielle's horses at the end of the month. They're moving over to the stable that hired Roy."

She sucked in a breath.

"I know—that was my reaction too." He ran a hand through his tousled hair. "We need a barn manager, Trisha. Someone our clients respect." He pierced her with a look. "Would you be willing to do it just for the summer?"

Her pulse quickened. When her fiancé's parents had pulled their offer to run their swanky horse stable at the same time Foster had dumped her, Trisha had lost confidence in her ability to manage a barn on her own. So when the Iowa teaching position had fallen into her lap, she'd jumped at the chance to move away from Texas and had firmly closed the door on running a barn.

That felt like a lifetime ago.

"I'm here for the kids, remember?" After her mother

had passed, her father, disinterested in parenting, had simply moved on with his life. She understood feeling abandoned, and she didn't want that for Sophie, Tommy or Gabby.

"Well, so far, the summer isn't turning out how any of us had hoped." His expression was so stoic, so sturdy. Parker and Avery had chosen the right person to take over the care of their children.

Her mind twirled at his request. "I don't know, Walker. There's got to be someone else."

He turned to her, the seriousness in his eyes almost scaring her. "Trisha, a housing developer put an offer on the property at the same time as Parker and Avery. The owners picked our friends because they planned on continuing the horse stable. Apparently, Silver Developers wanted to build homes on this land."

She gasped. "No."

"Yes. The developer contacted me the day of the closing and offered me almost double what we paid."

"But the kids."

"I know. Not only do we have to make this place profitable for them, if we fail, then Silver Developers may take over and change the landscape of Serenity." He rubbed the back of his neck, his face drawn in worry. "You went to college for ranch management, so if anyone can bring us out of the red, it's you." He placed his hand over hers and squeezed. "I promise you won't regret it."

At his touch, her pulse kicked up a notch. She slid her hand back into her lap and focused on the colorful sunset while pushing away the unwelcome attraction. Accepting the barn manager's position was a risky move. One she very well might regret. Unfortunately, she didn't seem to have much of a choice.

Her stomach rolled at the thought of losing this place to a land developer. Of not being able to let the kids live here like Parker and Avery had planned. They couldn't lose the farm, not after the kids had taken a giant step forward in their grieving process because of this move.

With two months before she returned to Iowa, the stable had to be running in tip-top shape so Walker could go back to his cybersecurity job when the kids returned to school. The only way to make that happen, and ensure the developers wouldn't get their greedy hands on the property, was to get back on track. That meant they needed a barn manager in place. Her stepping in for a short period made sense.

"Do you think I can do that work and still give the children enough time and attention?"

"That's probably a question parents ask themselves daily," he chuckled. "But seriously, acting as barn manager is what the children need so we can keep the farm, and I also think they'll enjoy being part of the daily operations."

She prayed for a moment and felt an immediate peace about accepting the position. "I have a couple of conditions. Rehire the groundskeeper and you take on the operations director role for the summer—you know, what the old owners used to do."

He held her gaze for a beat, then nodded. "Done." His quick decision to trust her warmed her heart.

"We both know Parker and Avery knew this farm would be a hard road financially, but they had faith that God would provide since they felt called to this life for their family."

Walker drew in a measured breath and then released

it before speaking. "I had no idea how tight it would end up being day to day."

"Most horse farms are, but this place takes it to a new level," she said as she eyed Walker and the passion he'd been showing in the daily operations here. "Who knows? You may find you can continue to do some tasks once you start your tech job back up," she said. "That way we could look for someone more qualified than, say, Roy to be the barn manager and do a few operations director tasks."

"So you'll do it?"

She gazed into his mesmerizing eyes. Working at the barn every day would put her in close proximity to Walker, and unfortunately, she found him attractive. But with her history of poor choices in men, he and all males were off-limits. Would helping turn the stable around be worth the risk of working so closely with him? It might not be easy, but she'd do it for the children. "Sure."

The anguish lining Walker's drawn face spoke to his genuine concern about the overconfident developer.

If we fail, then Silver Developers may take over and change the landscape of Serenity.

She lifted her chin. Somehow, they'd have to succeed.

Chapter Three

Friday morning, Trisha shifted her cowgirl hat to block the bright sun, grateful for the help of the feed store workers. "Thanks for loading those grain bags for me." In the back seat of the work pickup, the children's faces were pressed against the glass of the cab, engrossed in the workers' actions.

When finished, the store owner and his helpers tipped their worn Stetsons at Trisha. The two workers settled on the same rockers they'd been on when she'd arrived, one with a toothpick in the corner of his mouth and the other chewing on a fresh piece of straw.

If she weren't mistaken, all three older men had been here when she was in college and worked at the Triple C Ranch during the summers. She again wondered why Walker had gone to college when he'd had the opportunity of a lifetime at his family's ranch. The Triple C had just switched to grass-fed back then and she'd known they were going to make it big, and they had.

"We'll be on the lookout for a new barn manager and horse trainer for you," Cletus, the owner of the store, said.

"And spread the word about the open boarding spots at Serenity Stables."

At Cletus's kindness, tears sprang to her eyes. "We'd appreciate it." She slid into the driver's seat and glanced into the back. "All buckled?" Three excited nods. She'd only been here a week and yet it felt like home.

Trisha put the truck in Drive and headed to downtown Serenity. When she pulled into an angled parking spot in front of Wild Willie's Western Store, she noticed the ice cream shop next door. "After we pick out straw Stetsons and cowboy boots, how about some ice cream?" Sure, it was midmorning, but why not?

"Yes!" the kids stated in unison.

After their hats and boots purchase, and their cold treat from What's the Scoop, they piled back into the cab, happy and exhilarated. Trisha pointed the truck toward Serenity Stables.

"Walka never has the time to do things like this," Sophie stated from the back seat.

Hmm, maybe she'd have to encourage Walker to spend more quality time with the kids.

"Did you get the pretty pink jumpy castle?" Gabby asked, her eyes wide and sparkling as Trisha gazed at her in the rearview mirror.

"Sure did, honey," Trisha stated. "We're all set for next Saturday."

Gabby's eyes squinted with excitement. "I'm gonna be four."

She couldn't get over how Gabby had transformed from a little toddler to a big girl, right before her eyes. She'd been very clingy after her parents died, and it had continued nonstop. However, other than her clinginess the first few days after Trisha arrived, she'd been fine. Praise God.

Trisha smiled. "I can't believe it. I remember when you were born." Her voice caught, but she kept her smile in place. Trisha had been praying this milestone event wouldn't upset any of the children. A grief counselor had told her that all the firsts after the death of a loved one might trigger the kids to revert into one of the grieving stages. She prayed daily for each of them to move forward in their lives, yet remember details of their wonderful parents forever.

Back at the farm, a couple of boarders wearing velvet helmets were in the riding ring, jumping over cross-rails. They might have lost Bella and Arielle, but the other clients had stuck with them.

Walker came to help unload the grain, while Lilly Bug and Dip Dip ran out of the barn, nipping at one another's head.

The kids showed off their new attire, and Walker expressed the right amount of appreciation. Their excitement over such a small thing thrilled her.

The look of gratitude he flashed her way for outfitting them with cowboy garb made her senses spin. *Get a grip, Trisha. You're here for the kids, not some summer romance that will inevitably fail.* She took a step back, resolved not to let this attraction get out of hand.

"I'm going to give Treasure a sugar cube," Gabby announced. She trotted down the aisle, little hand clutching the tiny cube. Tommy and Sophie followed. The horses snorted and whinnied, trying to capture their attention.

"I've been looking around and we can get this feed much cheaper online." He paused at the back of the truck, his checked shirt doing nothing to hide the flexed muscles beneath.

Trisha cocked her head and took in his tall frame. "Walker, a small business needs to buy locally. Especially because we provide a service to the town." She tipped her cowboy hat back. "In fact, I talked with Cletus at the feed store and he and his employees said they'd pass the word that we need a barn manager and horse trainer. Oh, and that we have open stalls for boarding clients."

He stilled. The fifty-pound bag of grain sat on his strong shoulder like a light coat thrown there. "I hadn't considered that. Think it'll work?"

"In my experience, word of mouth is better than paid advertising."

They moved the bags of feed from the truck to the barn in silence.

She'd been the barn manager for only a handful of days, yet her confidence grew each day while her fear and uncertainty slowly fell away. Why had she allowed Foster's parents to get into her head and make her believe she couldn't do this job?

Amanda, their pert riding instructor, came to help, but Walker waved her off. As she turned away, she gave Walker a look of longing.

Jealousy flitted through Trisha. However, she refused to engage. The children needed a mother, and Trisha was a lost cause when it came to parenting.

"How about dating her?" Trisha pointed with her chin.

He kept his head down, Stetson covering his eyes as he ignored Amanda and trudged into the barn with another bag. "Nope. I'm off the dating circuit for good. Not after Phoebe," he said as his lips turned into a grim line. Losing his wife had left Walker downright grumpy. Though when Parker and Avery had passed and Walker needed to be there for the children, his attitude had turned around.

I'm off the dating circuit for good. Why? Probably because Phoebe had been the love of his life and he didn't want to sully her memory with a new wife.

The tips of his ears burned red. "I'm not sure why I just revealed that."

She wasn't either, but she liked that he was opening up to her. Yes, they were friends, although since college it had been more surface level than anything else. When Parker and Avery had died and she and Walker had been thrown together, they'd walked away from these past four months not only copartners in parenting but good friends as well.

He plopped the last bag of grain on the pile with a thwack, then turned and made his way down the corridor while she scurried to keep up. She had something important to discuss with him and he wasn't going to like it.

His comment about no dating meant he had no intention of ever remarrying. Why was Trisha's gut reaction relief? She should be concerned about the children. Instead, she was glad she wouldn't have to see a woman draped over Walker one day.

However, the kids deserved a complete family, as complete as they could get with their parents gone.

Riley Girl pushed her nose against Trisha's leg. She reached down to pet the dog and noticed she seemed rounder in the middle. Could Wilbur's dog be pregnant? Trisha loved having the older man and his Jacks around. He and his dogs had created a built-in homey environment for the children. Wilbur even had healthy snacks and drink pouches for the children when they stopped by his little cabin. She'd have to ask Wilbur if Riley Girl was expecting, because getting the children a pet, or pets, would be a great distraction against the loss of their parents.

Walker turned and speared her with that all-business look of his. "So, you're good at buying grain off the internet?"

She straightened at his absurd question. "Didn't you hear me, Walker, about the feed store?" She threw her hands out, exasperated. "We are a *local* business, so we need to reach our *local* customers."

"It's a ton cheaper online, though," he said through a clenched jaw.

"No. We need to support our local community. Period." She looked around to make sure no customers were within earshot and moved closer to him.

Alienating neighboring businesses was one great way to run the horse farm into the ground. She would not allow him to do that, but today she had more important things on her mind.

"Listen, Walker. I wanted you to know that the prior owners took a bunch of horses I was expecting they'd leave."

"They took horses that belong to us?" he asked as worry danced across his features.

"At first I thought so. You know how everything was a blur when Parker and Avery died, the memorial service, the kids, the decision to buy this place, getting others to handle my summer classes. I guess I just left the details to our Realtor. But last night I looked over the sales contract and it turns out they specified which horses they were taking and leaving, so everything looks fine to me."

His face fell, but she continued with her even worse news. "After talking with Amanda earlier, we don't have enough hacks to fulfill the existing lessons. She's had to split the larger group lessons in two to accommodate."

He rubbed the back of his neck. She could almost see the dollar signs flashing through his mind. "What are you saying?"

Even though he'd likely figured out where she was going, she had to say it out loud. "We're going to need to purchase at least four lesson horses at auction."

He groaned. "We don't have enough in the budget to buy the other horses you said we needed."

"Walker, you have to spend money to make money. If we don't have excellent horses to lease, we'll lose a pool of potential clients. Same goes for lesson horses."

He locked gazes with her, anxiety lacing his chocolate eyes. "You know this puts us in a graver financial situation, right?" he snapped at her.

Oh, she knew all right.

She had been the one to give the green light to proceed with the purchase of Serenity Stables. Had she made a rash decision?

Hopefully not, because the kids loved it here.

What would happen if this place was ripped away from them?

Gentle nickers came from the horses as Trisha made her way to the lower barn to deal with an issue after dropping that bombshell on him. Walker marched to his office with the swirling thought of defeat hanging in the humid air. The raw smells of leather and horseflesh infused the room.

He rubbed a hand over his face and closed the browsing tabs he'd opened to prove the grain was cheaper online. They had bigger issues to deal with, and frankly,

Trisha was right about buying right here in Serenity, where their customer pool lived. He certainly didn't want to alienate locals. But adding an additional expense for the auction would put them even more behind. The tab with the spreadsheet blinked at him. How could he get them out of the red?

He shook his head. No, out of the red wasn't good enough. His goal was to make this place profitable before the kids returned to school in September. But how could he do that and ensure Silver Developers wouldn't win?

Just this morning, Walker had believed they were on the right track. But now, with the additional money they needed to spend on lesson horses, he wasn't sure they could dig themselves out of this hole.

Wilbur lumbered by, holding Gabby's hand, likely telling her a story about growing up on Serenity Stables property. The kids were enthralled that the older man had once been as young as them. Riley Girl tagged close behind. It still made Walker a little nervous to have a stranger, and a pack of little dogs who thought they were big, living so close by, but Trisha and the children had taken to them like horseflies to a stallion. So, Walker hoped his worries were for naught.

Somewhere close by, he heard a surprised shriek from Sophie, chased by a sweet giggle that made him smile.

Trisha slid around the corner of the office, eyes down, a slip of paper in her hand. "I forgot to file the feed receipt," she said, her lips pursed. She slipped the sales receipt into the June accounts payable envelope and moved to leave.

"Trisha, wait." He took a cleansing breath while she settled against the door frame, the spray of freckles across her face more pronounced now that she'd been in the sun for a week. "I'm sorry for snapping about the extra expense of lesson horses and about Phoebe. There's just... a lot of stuff going on in here about her." He pointed to his thick skull.

Her stiff posture softened. Slightly. He'd take what he could get, considering that, for the kids, they were stuck together for many years to come.

She wouldn't make eye contact, but she twirled her hair around her index finger, which meant she was nervous. Now he felt horrible that he'd been sharp earlier. Somehow, he had to ease her discomfort.

"The groundskeeper agreed to come back," he told her. Something stirred in his belly at the bright smile that appeared on her face. Yes, he'd taken her suggestion and reached out to Archie, though he had no idea how they could afford the employee. "He'll be here early Monday."

She gave a little clap. "Thank you. I really like Archie."

She did? The idea of Trisha with Archie kicked him in the gut.

"You guys are the same age. Maybe you and he could date?" Wait. Why had he said that? It was the last thing he wanted. He shuffled the papers below his fingers as though looking for something.

Trisha took in a sharp breath. "For different reasons, I, too, am staying single." He detected a bit of hurt and bravado in her shaky voice. The glint that had occupied her midnight-green eyes had disappeared.

The knowledge that Trisha didn't want to date Archie, and didn't have a boyfriend back home waiting for her, caused something warm to wind around Walker's core.

Her fingers found her college ring and she worked it back and forth. Clearly, there was something more to staying single than she'd let on. Probably because Foster had called off the engagement mere weeks before the wedding. That would shake up anyone, but he'd thought she'd be over that by now.

"By the way, Sophie mentioned how much she enjoyed getting doughnuts the last couple of Saturdays. Good idea to splurge with the kids." As her eyes rested on him, they brightened, and she finally relaxed against the door frame. "Apparently, the complete experience of driving into town, waiting in line to pick her choice and getting a fancy beverage she rarely gets to drink was a lot of fun. She called it a new 'tradition.' Maybe we could do a couple more special things with the kids?"

"What were you thinking?"

"How about a kid-friendly movie on Friday nights? You know, pile on the couch and just watch a movie with popcorn?" Excitement hummed in the room at her idea.

"Maybe we could grab takeout too, let them eat in the living room during the movie?" He'd always thought it was special when his mom had let them eat on the couch.

"Ooh, I like that. Parker and Avery used to love Chinese takeout. Maybe we could do that?"

He nodded. "We could open the white boxes and let everyone take a little of everything."

"It's a date."

Just then, Sophie rounded the corner and stuck her head into the office. "You guys are going on a date?" The girl's excited gaze swung between the two of them.

Trisha wrapped her arms around the seven-year-old's shoulders and pressed a kiss to the top of her head. "No, sweetie, we were talking about watching a family movie tonight. All five of us."

Sophie looked at Trisha like she could walk on water.

"That sounds like such fun, Tish. Oh, thanks again for the ice cream, and hat and boots." She gave Walker a pointed look. "We're gonna play on the hay bale course until lunch." As quick as she'd come, she left. Lilly Bug and Dip Dip raced after her, yipping for attention.

"Why did Sophie give me that look?" he asked. "What'd I do?"

"She mentioned you never take the time to do things with them. You're always working. Apparently, something like stopping for ice cream or picking up boots and hats are things they've asked you to do, but you've said you don't have the time."

He let her harsh, yet true, words sink in. Trisha was right. He was the worst guardian ever.

On the other hand, she connected with each of the kids where they were. She put them at ease and filled their mom hole.

The kids really needed her, especially because he wasn't much to write home about.

Trisha leaned across the desk and touched his arm, quickly pulling her fingers back as though he had an infectious disease. "Don't go thinking you aren't a suitable guardian. You are amazing." Her kind words circled through him and gave him the encouragement to keep trying.

Heat flushed her cheeks as she looked away. Her clean scent filled the tiny office space and he leaned forward for one more breath.

"It's just that you may want to stop and smell the roses, so to speak," she said.

But his mind was stuck on her prior praise. She thought he was amazing. He'd hold on to that compliment. "I'll try."

Something shifted in his chest. He wasn't sure what, but having someone like her in his corner gave him hope that maybe the next few months wouldn't be as over- whelming with Trisha by his side.

A warm breeze from the open window tousled her hair and she gathered her locks to one side, exposing the length of her neck. He couldn't look away.

"Not that I should be speaking." She rushed on, worry- ing her dainty hands. "I mean, I had an absent father and no mother, so you shouldn't be quick to take advice from me. Lunch is in fifteen." As abruptly as she'd arrived, Trisha turned on her heel and started back to the house.

"Wait."

She swiveled, her lips flattened in a tight line. She lifted her chin in question, and he wanted to rub away the worry lines on her forehead.

Stop. What was he thinking?

"I'm not hungry today, but thanks." He gulped. There was no way he could sit at the table across from her right now. This attraction bubbling up between them had to end, because the guilt that came with it was creating a burning pit in his stomach.

"Whatever." She marched off.

He pushed away her disappointment as the sweet scent of fresh hay drifted into the office. Buck must be feed- ing the horses their lunch.

Fifteen minutes later, Sophie ran into the office with a bulging brown bag that smelled suspiciously of ham and mustard. His stomach growled.

"Tish wanted you to have this. Gotta go." Sophie planted a soft kiss on his cheek and rushed back to the house. Most likely to her lunch at the sunny kitchen table surrounded by her rowdy and adorable siblings. He made a mental note to stop and smell the roses, as Trisha had recommended. These children had lost so much, they deserved more from him, and since quality time was free, it was something he could give them.

He opened the bag and pulled out two sandwiches, an overstuffed baggie filled with potato chips, and three dill pickles wrapped in plastic wrap. Yum.

His heart swelled that Trisha had thought of him and was smart enough to realize he had fibbed when he'd stated he wasn't hungry, because he was famished. Perhaps she'd thought he had too much work to do and didn't have time for a lunch break. Regardless, he was confident she didn't feel the romance brewing between them, because there was none. There couldn't be.

The dogs yipped in the distance, then quieted.

Now he felt bad he had brought up dating Archie. Even though Walker would never marry again, never be in love again, he wanted the best for Trisha. Whatever that might look like for her.

She'd probably be surprised he found her attractive. She was also funny and completely perfect as a mother figure for the children, no matter what her past.

Woe! He jumped up from the chair, half-eaten sandwich in hand. No, she couldn't be more than a friend—and even *friend* felt a bit precarious.

Nope, after what had happened with Phoebe, he wasn't worthy of a chance at love again.

And, frankly, any woman deserved more than him.

"Boss," Ryder said as he leaned around the door frame. "A couple of guys are sniffing around. They have suits on."

Suits?

He put his sandwich down and hurried out to see what

they wanted. A man crouched low beside the riding ring, the other suit standing beside him with a glass tube.

The hairs on the back of Walker's neck rose. "Can I help you?"

The standing suit grinned. "I'm King. This is Falcon. We're with Silver Developers," he said as he offered his hand. "Just testing the soil."

Walker swallowed hard and ignored his extended hand. "This is private property."

King nodded as Falcon stood and deposited dirt into the glass tube. "We get that, but we just want to get ahead of the curve."

Falcon capped the tube and slid it into a labeled plastic bag.

"What's that mean?"

"We want to be ready when you admit defeat and sell. Have a good day." The two left as swiftly as they'd appeared.

A vise tightened around Walker's chest at Silver Developers' confidence, and he could barely breathe.

Somehow, he and Trisha needed to turn this horse farm around. For the children.

Chapter Four

Rain pattered on the barn windows Monday morning as Walker stared at the bottom of the accounting software screen and the blinking red number. How had they gone from barely in the black when they'd purchased the place to in the red that fast? He laced his fingers behind his head and leaned back in the office chair. Maybe they shouldn't have purchased those lesson horses at the auction. So what if they had to split classes in two? Paying their riding instructor more would be cheaper than those four new hacks. He glanced at the screen again. The numbers didn't even reflect the salaries for the barn manager or horse trainer.

A groan slipped from his lips at the overwhelming situation. Silver Developers was looking more promising by the day, but no, he would not sell. The children and the community deserved better.

"What's wrong?" Trisha popped into the tiny office and palmed her cowboy hat.

Teamwork, Walker. Somehow, he had to wrap his brain around working with her instead of going off on his own, like he usually did, to solve problems.

"How are we going to get the operation in the black by September, when we both return to our jobs?" he blurted.

Her brows furrowed in concern as she took a tentative step into the office.

"We've just had a hiccup with purchasing horses we hadn't budgeted for." Her calm voice soothed him, unlike anyone else. Before he knew it, she moved away and out of sight.

He gazed up at the wood rafters. Was she right? Were these just onetime expenses they'd bounce back from? He focused on the screen and plugged in some new numbers. If they expanded their boarding by several horses, leased both new horses out, and increased their lessons by like double, then added in a barn manager's salary, he could nudge the bottom line into a black number. But that sounded impossible.

The old-school barn phone rang. He picked up the black-corded receiver, surprised to hear Mrs. Hudson on the line.

"After chatting with Trisha at the consignment store over the weekend, I've changed my mind about pulling our horses," Mrs. Hudson stated. "We're going to continue boarding at Serenity Stables, assuming you haven't already booked our stalls."

Walker grinned. "No, we have space for Scout and Lady." *Yes!* He fist-pumped his excitement. The quarter horses would stay. The phone slipped from his shoulder. He righted it.

Mrs. Hudson sighed with relief. "I'm thrilled to hear that. Also, Bella and Arielle want to increase their lessons to twice a week. Could you accommodate that?"

"Absolutely. I'll have Amanda call to schedule a time."

"My husband wanted to verify that you have liability

insurance," she said, then rushed on. "I'm sure you do, but I had to ask."

His excitement quickly turned to unease. Had Trisha hooked them up? He sure hadn't thought about insurance in the hectic month since the purchase. "We are in the middle of firming that up right now, Mrs. Hudson. No worries."

A relieved breath sounded over the line before she thanked him and ended the call.

His pulse pounded in his ears at the insurance issue. Maybe Trisha had taken care of it?

But Scout and Lady were staying, and Bella and Arielle were increasing their lessons. He let out a hoot of excitement. Roy leaving had bummed him out, but now he saw how God had Walker's back. Maybe God had known all along that Trisha would need to step in as barn manager to get a handle on things.

Though, he had to talk with Trisha about the liability insurance right away.

His gaze flashed to the screen. Two boarders not leaving didn't change the facts. Somehow, the farm had to become self-sufficient.

When Trisha went back to Iowa and he returned to his computer career, they'd have to pay a salary for barn manager, horse trainer and operations director. He had placed his career on hold when Parker and Avery had passed. But "on hold" might quickly turn into a dead career if he didn't stay current with the training and new technologies. A hard knot settled in Walker's chest.

"What was all that noise about?" Trisha wiped a bead of sweat from her brow.

"Mrs. Hudson changed her mind about Scout and Lady.

They're staying. Also, the girls are now scheduled for two lessons a week instead of one."

She clapped and grinned. "Yay, I'm so thrilled."

Boy, she was cute.

"Thank you for reaching out to her."

She waved her hand dismissively at him. "It was no biggie."

He wiggled his fingers to invite her in. "Can you close the door?"

Worry swept over her features.

He explained the liability insurance Mrs. Hudson had asked about. When her face fell, he knew Parker's and Avery's sudden deaths, the orphaned children and the decision to go ahead with the purchase had overwhelmed them both, not leaving them with enough bandwidth to remember some of the little things.

"Okay, I'll call my insurance adjuster today and get a quote," he said, though he knew it would not be a small number and that it would be an ongoing expense, but one they must have.

The air felt heavy as she opened the door and disappeared from his view.

He got up to stretch and then followed her into the stable.

She walked down the concrete aisle and horses neighed and lifted their heads to get her attention, but she ignored them. Her silky auburn hair bounced against her back with each step she took. She untied Goliath, a giant mean gelding, from the cross-hook and headed toward the pastures. The rain had ended, and the sun was now peeking out. A nearby horse kicked its stall door, causing Goliath to skitter away, but Trisha firmly led him out.

She rounded the corner and slipped from sight, planning to let the mean horse have the far right pasture all to himself, where he wouldn't hurt anyone. Goliath was the one horse Walker wished they hadn't inherited. No one could ride him and he was a menace to the other animals.

"He's got some good in him," Wilbur said, startling Walker. "I just don't think anyone's dug deep enough to find it yet."

Walker gave the older man a long look. Even in the heat of the summer, he wore his usual overalls and flannel shirt. "Trisha thinks so too." Skeeter and Riley Girl both jumped against Walker's legs, looking for a treat or maybe some affection. He leaned down and absently scratched the scruff of their necks while the call to the insurance adjuster weighed on his mind.

"He's only been here a few months, and no one really gave him a chance."

Walker rubbed his tired eyes. "Well, with the kids around, Goliath makes me pretty nervous. Can you think of anyone who'd be willing to take him off our hands?"

"Prior owners already tried that." Wilbur shuffled his feet, his worn boots seemingly about ready to give up the ghost. "Say, Trisha's proving herself to be pretty invaluable, huh?"

"She is." They couldn't afford a new barn manager right now, and to be honest, Trisha was good. He headed back to his office.

Walker might have just bought himself a whole heap of trouble, because when they'd gone through with the purchase of Serenity Stables, the plan hadn't involved the two of them working so closely together. It was supposed to be Walker getting this place off the ground, except he couldn't envision the place running in the black without her here.

He shook the unwanted feelings aside and sucked in air mingled with the scent of sawdust to loosen the thick emotions stuck in his throat.

What he really wanted was an older man to step in as barn manager. Someone who didn't entice him and make him dream of moving on with his life. Make him believe he deserved a second shot at love, which he knew he didn't.

"Tommy, no!" Trisha's sharp voice yelled from a distance.

Walker's heart jumped into his throat as he rushed to the pastures, sending a pleading prayer for Tommy's safety. His mind was firmly on Goliath and his over one thousand pounds. He tried not to consider what damage the gelding could unknowingly do to a small child.

Sure enough, Tommy motored his bicycle in the south corner of the pasture, mud splattering behind his thick tires. The boy was at Goliath's back, but what if the gelding turned around and charged? He added his voice to the mix of warnings, but with a helmet on, Tommy likely couldn't hear them shouting. The boy was so used to wearing a helmet, from when they'd lived in town, that he continued the practice here at the farm.

Trisha raced along the fence line toward the giant horse. What was she doing? The horse, innocently grazing, might startle at her appearance and kick her. Maybe trample her.

"Trisha, stop!" he yelled.

Tommy must have seen Trisha, because he turned around and raced out of the pasture to safety. *Thank You, Lord.*

As Walker came to the spot where he'd have to decide if he should enter the pasture or not, his lungs burned.

Trisha slowed to a walk and approached Goliath, her boots sinking into the mud. Now that Tommy was safe, why wasn't she turning and fleeing?

Almost in slow motion, Goliath turned and threw his head back at Trisha's appearance. Then he reared up, his strong hooves covered in mud, but she didn't move. Her hands were out, and Walker could hear her speaking soothing words to the gelding.

Get out, he wanted to scream. Instead, he stood stock-still and watched, unable to do a thing to help or save her.

Goliath's front feet landed close to Trisha, his nostrils angrily flaring in her face. The gelding had the chance to trample her if he wanted.

Lord, please keep Trisha safe. Give her wisdom on how to get out of there without getting hurt. Lay Your calming hand on Goliath.

Then Trisha leaned her forehead against the bridge of the horse's nose.

Sweat ran into Walker's eyes as he continued to pray for her safety, unable to do a thing.

Goliath lifted his head a few times in resistance, but then the giant pawed his right hoof once, slinging mud behind him, and stilled. He even started to close his eyelids.

Walker's tight chest loosened. She really was a horse whisperer.

But that feeling of helplessness he'd had when Goliath had reared up was the exact reason he couldn't get involved with anyone ever again. There was no way he'd allow himself to care for someone again and lose.

There was no way he could go through that loss again.

Later in the day, Trisha stood in front of the huge calendar hanging from two nails and ran her finger along the Wednesday riding lessons. She couldn't get the cozy Friday evening watching the Disney movie and eating Chinese takeout out of her mind. The kids had loved it. Sophie had danced around the house singing about their new Friday movie night tradition. But the part that had surprised Trisha was her reaction to sitting next to Walker. Soon after they'd finished eating, Gabby had laid her head on Trisha's lap and Walker had scooted over so he could stroke the girl's back. Even though Gabby had fallen fast asleep, Walker had remained close during the entire movie.

She had liked it.

"I heard about Goliath and Tommy," Amanda said, as she came out of the tack room with a bridle hanging on her arm.

Trisha felt a flush crawl up her neck at the image of Friday evening.

"Good job." Amanda nodded, referring to Goliath. Not Walker and their closeness during the movie.

Trisha switched gears to Goliath's behavior earlier. The moment she had spotted Tommy zipping along on his bike and dashing under the fence into Goliath's pasture, she'd started running for the rescue. When Tommy hadn't responded to her repeated yells of his name, she'd known she'd have to get in Goliath's face or something terrible might happen to little Tommy. She would never allow that on her watch.

"Apparently, Tommy got himself to safety before I reached Goliath, but I'm glad I connected with the gelding. He needs someone to believe in him."

Amanda whistled. "Believe? Huh, that guy needs a world of work. But if you think you can break him, go for it." The riding instructor wasn't convinced Goliath could become a safe horse to be around, and Trisha intended to prove her wrong.

Amanda's face turned serious. "Does this have anything to do with what you were telling Sophie? About losing your mom young and having your father focus on everything but you?"

A lump formed in Trisha's throat. Normally she didn't share, but to help Sophie, she'd do just about anything. "Kind of."

"It's great what you and Walker are doing for the kids. Not just the horse farm, but being there for them." She pointed to the wall-mounted calendar. "Whatcha doin' here?"

Trisha focused on the reason she'd come to this part of the barn. "Can you do a group class on Wednesday evenings about seven?" At Amanda's nod, she continued. "I was in town over the weekend and bumped into several people and touted our boarding and lessons. But I realized we were missing the market by not offering adult classes. Primarily moms who may want to take a group lesson once a week. I could advertise it as a mom's night out."

Amanda smiled. "That's brilliant. But maybe six thirty? That way, Dad can clean up from dinner and get the kids ready for bed, but Mom is home in time for the bedtime story."

"I like how you think."

"I have a sister with two little ones. Their schedule is their lifeline."

Trisha penciled in a new lesson for Wednesday evenings, already considering ways to market the class. This wouldn't be a huge income for the farm, but every bit helped. Somehow, they'd have to become profitable and get this place running smoothly before she returned to Iowa in September.

"Up to no good?"

Trisha startled at Walker's words. "Drumming up business, boss." She told him about her idea while Amanda, with a pensive look on her face, leaned against the stall.

She loved how Walker's brow became uncreased when he heard the plan. Somehow, she felt like he made her a better person by just being himself. His encouraging words always made her want to please him again.

"Pretty and smart."

Amanda cleared her throat. "While I have the two of you here." She tugged the corner of her lip with her teeth, as though agitated. Trisha and Walker exchanged a nervous look. Amanda wasn't quitting, was she?

But thankfully, she only wanted to make her case to add the part-time horse trainer position to her plate. Because she waitressed part-time in the evenings to make ends meet, and didn't even make minimum wage, she'd be happy with any increase they gave her.

Relief coursed through Trisha at Amanda's request. She glanced at Walker and he nodded. "Amanda, that'd be great. I don't know why we didn't think of that."

She gave Amanda a side hug, and their new horse trainer headed down the aisle with her tack, head held a little higher.

As they high-fived, Trisha grinned at Walker. Before she could linger and enjoy his spicy scent, he told her how much the liability insurance would cost them. Even if they completely filled the new class they'd just decided to start, it wouldn't come close to covering the unexpected expense.

"What are we going to do?" Despair laced her tone at the rhetorical question.

He shrugged as the offer from Silver Developers lay between them, though the housing developer was not an option.

Motion from the parking lot caught her attention. The woman from church had arrived for the tour. Trisha shook off the up-and-down emotions of the last thirty minutes and greeted the potential client as she stepped into the barn. "Norma, I'm glad you could come. This is Walker McCaw. He handles everything around here."

They shook hands, and then Norma introduced them to Gemma, her teenage daughter.

Trisha shouldn't feel so pleased at the glint of appreciation in Walker's eyes. When they met at the consignment store the other day, Norma had asked what had brought her to town and the stable tour organically came up. Trisha hadn't been trying to drum up business—it just seemed to keep finding her.

With a last look of thankfulness on his face, Walker excused himself.

Yesterday, sitting on the hard pew listening to the sermon, Trisha hadn't been able to get her mind off why she had lost everyone she loved. Her mother had died on her. Her father had never treated her as a priority. Foster had dumped her like a cold potato.

Was she so terribly flawed that she was unlovable? Frankly, even God seemed far away.

"Thanks for making time for us today," Norma said. "I'm sure you're super busy."

Not nearly as busy as she'd like. "Happy to help. I think Serenity Stables will be a good fit. It's smaller and cozier than where you are."

A horse nickered somewhere down the aisle and another echoed in response.

As she showed them the stalls, Lilly Bug and Dip Dip scrambled toward them. Trisha leaned down and kept them from jumping on the visitors. Both Norma and her daughter seemed excited with the space, commenting on how the stalls were larger than where they were boarding now.

They walked out of the barn, the Jack Russells close behind, and Trisha pointed out the pastures. The tall grasses blew in the warm June breeze.

Norma's face glowed as she and her daughter wandered the path between the pastures and talked. Trisha felt like she had this deal in the bag. Her phone buzzed with an incoming text.

When can we meet? The app isn't letting me schedule an appointment and I need to talk!

An ache pierced her chest at the distress in Lauren's message. She'd been the student's mentor and had helped her secure the summer position at a mega stable where she was shadowing the barn manager, Lauren's dream job upon graduation. She'd been there for the bright girl for three years and didn't want to disappoint the student now.

I'm out of town for the summer. What can I help you with?

As Trisha hit Send, she knew she was failing the girl. Lauren was smart, but also craved guidance. Unlike her contemporary college students, texting or video chatting wasn't Lauren's modus operandi. She enjoyed meeting in person.

The little reply bubble danced on her screen while Trisha impatiently waited for Lauren to compose her reply. But no text came through.

"What's next?" Norma asked.

"We have one outdoor riding ring." Trisha shoved her phone in her back pocket as she tried to put the urgency of Lauren's needs behind her for the moment. She pointed at the outdoor ring and gave her spiel about the space. Though Walker had dragged it this morning to smooth the surface of the sand, many riders had ridden today, so it wasn't as neat as she had hoped it would be.

The utility vehicle sat on the far side of the ring, where Walker was helping Archie replace a couple of rotted boards. He removed his Stetson, lifted his head, and their gazes met. Her heart raced at Walker's attention. *Calm down, Trisha. He's only a friend.*

She twisted her hands and studied him across the expanse of land. No. He didn't want a relationship with anyone, and neither did she. The past had burned them both.

She shook off the thoughts and pointed to the building beside the gravel parking lot. "Our indoor ring is over there, complete with a viewing room. Would you like to see it?"

Norma nodded and the trio began walking. Right then, Trisha's phone buzzed with another incoming text. She pulled it out.

Things aren't going the way I'd hoped and I need to talk. Will you be back for a weekend soon?

I'm sorry, but I won't be back until after Labor Day.

September??? Noooooo.

An invisible fist squeezed the breath out of Trisha's lungs at how she was disappointing the girl. Yes, she was duty bound to be in Serenity. The farm, the kids, even Walker, needed her. But at this moment, her heart was back in Iowa with Lauren and the other students she'd grown so fond of through the years.

How about we video chat?

The dreaded three dots danced again, with no immediate reply. She was letting the girl down and it tore her apart.

I guess so...

The discouraged answer caused frustration to build in Trisha's chest because she couldn't physically be there for Lauren. They set a time to video chat and Trisha pocketed her phone.

How could Trisha feel pulled in two separate directions? Both good. Both noble. Both felt so right. She hoped she didn't have to make a choice about which life to lead, because she wasn't sure she could say no to either.

"Did I tell you how much of a curmudgeon Roy was?" Norma interrupted her thoughts as the older lady's nose scrunched up like she was smelling fresh horse manure. "I mean, we live on the outskirts of Serenity, but we've been traveling two towns away to board Gemma's horse the past few years."

"I'm glad I ran into you over the weekend, then. Sounds like Serenity Stables will be much more convenient."

They toured the indoor ring, and then Trisha quoted the monthly rate.

"That's lower than we're paying. We'll take it."

After they hashed out the details of the transport, Norma hugged Trisha. "I can't thank you enough. If it weren't for you, there's no way we'd make this change. As you know, the barn manager is key to a successful boarding situation." The pair climbed into their truck.

Trisha broke out in a nervous sweat as Norma's words rang out in her mind. *The barn manager is key to a successful boarding situation.*

She gulped. If she went back to Iowa and Walker returned to his cybersecurity job, no one with a personal stake in the operation's success would be here every day. And after communicating with Lauren today, she knew she wasn't ready to give up her Iowa life just yet.

Walker's fear of failing might come true if they didn't have someone with a personal stake in the daily operations. If they failed, the kids wouldn't be able to grow up here like their parents had desired and Silver Developers would take over and change the landscape of Serenity, Texas.

Chapter Five

Saturday morning, a man in a bright orange shirt pressed a button, and the rented bounce house expanded and took shape.

"It's so pwetty," Gabby whispered over the low buzzing noise from the machine. She rose onto her toes in excitement.

Trisha grinned and wrapped her arms around the girl's shoulders to stop her from getting tangled with the bounce house.

The bright pink turrets of the structure popped up, and Gabby sucked in a breath. "I love it." She squeezed Trisha's leg. "This is going to be the bestest birthday party ever."

Well, at least Trisha had gotten this right. Because last night at bedtime, Tommy had pushed her away and refused to listen to a story. Informed her he was too old for that baby stuff.

So she'd given him a quick hug, told him she loved him and left his room. But it had still hurt.

She knew he was probably acting out because he missed his parents. When Walker had joined her on the porch, they'd prayed for all the kids to get through this first birthday party without too much sadness.

Now she kissed the top of Gabby's head, her wispy hair tickling Trisha's nose.

She loved the kids so much that when they hurt, she hurt. Thankfully, Tommy was acting absolutely normal this morning. He'd climbed onto her lap for his brief morning cuddle time and had seemed chipper and upbeat about the day ahead, even though they had stayed up later than expected last night. The family movie they'd picked had been longer than she had anticipated, so she was grateful the kids weren't cranky today. At least, not yet.

As soon as the buzzing stopped, the man in orange waved to her and Gabby raced to the castle.

Shielding her eyes from the midmorning sun, Trisha watched Gabby take those first few jumps. When the girl slid down the slide and shrieked in delight, Trisha laughed. Static electricity caused Gabby's baby-fine hair to stand straight up in the air.

Trisha turned to get the space ready for guests. As she worked on decorating the tables, she breathed in the freshly mowed grass mixed with the distinct aroma of horse.

A few hours later, after taping the paper tablecloths to the tables Walker had set up, and fixing everything just so, the guests started arriving. She greeted Walker's parents and then Autumn.

"Trisha, everything looks great," Autumn said as she hugged her. "What can I do?"

For starters, make your brother less appealing to me. She straightened. Hopefully, she hadn't said that out loud. "Maybe greet guests? Show them where the gift and buffet tables are?" She gazed at the short-cropped field filled with children already running around, screams emitting from the active bouncy castle.

"Everyone has that under control, Trisha." Her friend pointed at the well-organized tables and the camp chairs people had brought and set up.

It hadn't taken long for the gift table to overflow with presents for the birthday girl and guests to place covered dishes on the buffet table to go along with the hamburgers Walker planned to grill. "Maybe they've done this a time or two?"

Most get-togethers Trisha had attended, guests didn't bring food to share or chairs for themselves. She smiled at the scene before her. Why had she worried about the details when all everyone needed was a field to hang out in and the party girl to celebrate?

"Thanks for helping us move the horses around the other night," Trisha said.

"Happy to help. I think it's smart to have the boarded and leased horses in one barn to give the riders a better sense of community. You've got some great ideas."

She waved a hand as though shooing away a fly. "It's a team effort." She spotted Wilbur, with his Kiss the Cook apron on, talking to a group of older men. He held a spatula, as though waiting for Walker to call all the cooks to their grills. "Wilbur's stronger than he looks."

"He was so helpful the other night." Autumn giggled. "It tuckered me out when we were done, and he still seemed pretty fresh."

Trisha was thankful for the older man. He'd become a friend to her and the kids, and Walker was warming up to him.

"The kids seem to be doing well. I know you were

worried about taking over the barn manager role." Autumn cocked her head.

"They each seem motivated to help and learn, and they absolutely love being with the horses all day."

"Good. I think it helps that you know what they're going through because you lost your mom."

"I'm not sure how much of a help I am since I was never my mother's priority or my father's," she said as she eyed Walker by the bounce house. "You know what I really wish? I wish I'd finally be someone's priority." She glanced around to make sure no one could hear them. "I just want someone to tell me that I am worthy of their time and attention, you know what I mean?" Her throat clogged and her eyes burned. She blinked the tears away.

"Oh, honey." Autumn gave her a side hug. "If I'm not mistaken, there may be someone who already feels that way."

Why had she stated her dream out loud? She gave a shake of her head. "No. That's not what I meant." But no matter what she said to backpedal, Autumn had that matchmaking look in her eye.

Trisha stepped away to straighten the gifts as Autumn turned to answer a question Laney, her sister-in-law, had asked.

Walker strolled over, and her breath stalled in her lungs. With his hands tucked into his pristine jeans' pockets, and a new black T-shirt stretched across his chest, she resisted lifting a hand to fan her face. How was the simple presence of him able to turn Trisha's thoughts and emotions upside down?

She focused on Gabby, and her happy, sweaty little face, in the bounce castle.

"Can I help with anything?" His deep timbre drew

Trisha to him and made her insides do somersaults. His dark hair and tanned skin set off his breathtaking chocolate eyes. *What is happening?*

She'd sworn off men. All men. Even if a relationship started, Walker would quickly realize Trisha didn't have worth and he'd leave like everyone else.

She lifted her chin and pushed her romantic feelings away. "Maybe start the grill."

Just then, Henry Wright stepped up to Walker, almost nose to nose.

"I hear some housing developer is sniffing around and you're close to selling," he stated, louder than Trisha would have liked.

Many people turned their way. Cora held on to her husband's arm as though holding him back from trying to come over and fight their fight.

"No," Walker stated calmly. "We don't plan to sell." His statement broke Trisha's heart because she knew how close they were to losing the farm.

A thick vein in Henry's neck pulsed as the two had a stare-down. "You better not. It'd ruin Serenity." Henry jutted his chin and strutted off toward the edge of the camp chairs, where his wife drew him in. She whispered something to him. He nodded and then hung his head as though in defeat.

Walker stalked off toward the grills while Trisha turned and made a beeline for Autumn, her safety net.

Soon, the appealing smell of grilling hamburgers scented the air. Her stomach growled and she forced herself to forget about Henry's mean comments and how close they truly were to caving in and selling to Silver Developers.

For a moment, Trisha paused and took in the chatter.

A group of young moms caught her attention, so Trisha settled in the chair beside Autumn's and soaked in the loving atmosphere. The women appeared to have long-lasting bonds with each other. They shared life together. Trisha's heartbeat quickened.

Sure, she had friends back in Iowa. Kind of. But this was different. There wasn't competition, just encouragement. She never thought she'd wanted close female companionship, but in this moment she craved to be a genuine part of this group. Forever. She wanted to get to know these women better. To share a lifelong bond with them.

Except she couldn't have this life. She had worked hard for her career in academia. She had even received a promotion at the end of the school year, one she'd been working hard and praying for. She leaned back in her camp chair and took in the family environment.

Many of the parents were sitting and chatting, but the ones who were standing and watching the kids playing, chasing and bouncing seemed to have worked out shifts with each other. Occasionally, a couple would wander back to their seats and another couple would hop up and take their place. The adage *it takes a village* popped into Trisha's head. She loved that Gabby, Tommy and Sophie had an entire community, not just her and Walker, to care for them. Raise them. Correct them. Love them.

"Everyone." Wade raised his voice so the crowd could hear him. "Let's gather around to pray for our food and this sweet four-year-old that God has given us."

The guests quieted for Walker's dad.

"Lord, be with Gabby today as she celebrates her birthday. Thank You for being her Heavenly Father and always loving her…" he started.

But the rest of the words just blurred as Wade's first

few sentences soaked into Trisha's soul. They reminded her that just because her earthly mother had died and her earthly father had been disinterested didn't mean that God had forsaken her. Just because Foster had broken up with her mere weeks before their wedding and turned her life upside down, God had always remained steadfast.

Frankly, Trisha was the one who'd elevated herself over God when she'd moved to Iowa. She had believed that since Foster had considered her unworthy of marrying, God might regard her as unsuitable as well.

Why had she given Foster so much power?

When the prayer ended, many people stood to fill their plate while Trisha looked around for the kids. Tommy and Gabby were in the bounce house, but where was Sophie? As she walked closer to the bounce structure, she scanned the field. The seven-year-old was nowhere to be found. Trisha circled the bounce castle. No Sophie.

She went to the house, opened the front door and heard a faint noise from upstairs. She rushed up the stairs and heard sobbing coming from Sophie's room. Gently, she pushed open the bedroom door.

Sophie lay on her stomach, head in her hands, weeping.

The sound made Trisha feel powerless. Was this how parents felt? She reached out to rub Sophie's back, but the girl pushed her hand away.

Trisha's fingertips itched to help. Instead, she sidled up next to her on the bed. Before she could say an encouraging word, Sophie cut her off.

"Go away," Sophie wailed.

Trisha's heart shattered at Sophie's sadness and her inability to fix things, or at least make her feel better.

So she did the only thing she could. She closed her

eyes and prayed for the girl. That the crying would help Sophie close another chapter of her grieving. That all the kids would know she and Walker were here for them forever. It felt good to rely solely on God.

Sophie continued weeping, but the sobs seemed a bit more controlled as the minutes passed.

Parenting was hard work. But this? This was simply gut-wrenching.

Trisha clasped her hands and prayed a little more.

Last night, when Tommy had acted out, it had seemed natural. As though he'd missed his parents on the eve of their first birthday celebration without Parker and Avery. Likely, Sophie was upset for the same reason.

Sophie's sobs turned into whimpers, but that didn't make Trisha feel any better.

The helplessness tore at her gut.

No. She was not fit to parent anyone, especially these three sweet children.

The next afternoon, the dark clouds from earlier drifted away as filtered light streamed across the pastures. The property looked much tidier with their groundskeeper back on the job, but still there was a never-ending list of tasks to accomplish.

"I have a ton on my plate. Why don't you take the kids?" Walker asked Trisha as she confidently slipped into the passenger seat of the utility terrain vehicle.

Trisha leaned in and whispered, "Stop and smell the roses." Too quickly, she moved away and eyed him. "The work will wait for your return. Anyway, we unloaded the leased horses from auction and Ryder can settle them in just fine." Her natural scent tickled his nose and stirred up a longing for a companion again.

He stepped back. Okay, now he had two reasons not to go on this little excursion. Except her rebuke hit exactly where she'd hoped—his heart. He gazed at the excitement on Sophie's and Tommy's faces. Trisha was right. He needed to make time for these kids, to make memories, as Trisha kept saying.

"She's right, ya know," Wilbur said. "And I'm here if anyone needs anything."

Two weeks ago, Walker would have laughed at the older man's comment, but not anymore. Wilbur knew the comings and goings of this place and was super protective of the horses and the children. For that, Walker was forever grateful. The man had grown on him and now he couldn't imagine Serenity Stables without Wilbur.

Last night, Wilbur had invited them for s'mores over the firepit. Shockingly, he had an expansive backyard with an amazing view of the distant pond, probably because his little piece of property was on a rise. Even more surprising was how Sophie and Tommy tag-teamed to tell "Chief," as they called him, about how their parents had chosen Serenity Stables as the place for them to live. That they'd toured the property with their parents before their deaths and talked about the future, and how much they loved living here. Neither had broken down while talking about their mom and dad, though Gabby had crawled into Trisha's lap and sucked her thumb while listening. But the little girl had slept great last night, no nightmares.

The emotional success of the children gave Walker even more incentive to make sure they turned the farm around so the children could stay.

"I'll be right back," Trisha stated when Ryder motioned for her.

As Trisha went over to confer with Ryder, Wilbur spoke. "Have you seen Trisha working with Goliath?" Respect glinted in the older man's eyes.

"Absolutely." The enormous horse had changed a ton in just a week. He couldn't imagine how tame he would become by the time Trisha returned to Iowa.

Wilbur chuckled. "She has a soft spot for Goliath. Trisha's theory is you have to love the horse, not just the ride."

"What does that mean?"

"Everyone wants to ride the well-mannered horse that wins ribbons in shows. But the Goliaths of this world are shunned because they weren't properly schooled." He re-settled his worn Stetson. "All Goliath needs is love and acceptance, and to be taught right from wrong. Then he'll be winning at horse shows before you know it. You just watch."

Well, that sounded impossible, because no one could even place a saddle on the giant. But if Trisha could make Goliath no longer a danger to those around him, Walker would be pleased.

As Trisha returned and collected the children like a mother hen, the older kids scrambled into the back seat and Gabby settled between them in the front. Wilbur waved as they took off, his four Jack Russell terriers standing beside him.

"Bye, Chief," they sang to him.

Walker wasn't sure where the nickname had come from, but it had stuck. Regardless, he liked the sound of having a chief watching out for him and the kids. It reminded him that God was always by his side.

Walker pressed the gas pedal and the utility vehicle zipped down the dirt path, pastures on each side. He held tight to his Stetson to keep the breeze from snatching it off his head. When he got to the edge of the pastures, he slowed so the children and Trisha could view the property they hadn't yet seen.

"Texas bluebells." Trisha pointed to the sprawling field of green sprinkled with bluish-purple flowers.

"Can we stop and pick them?" Sophie asked.

After Walker eased the vehicle to a stop, the kids piled out. The girls rushed to pick the flowers. Tommy tagged after them, his hands shoved in his pockets, but quickly moved to Gabby and pushed her to the ground.

Trisha popped up and rushed over, making sure Gabby wasn't hurt. Then she took Tommy's hands.

"Tommy, apologize to Gabby," Trisha said, her voice stern yet loving. "That wasn't a kind or loving thing to do."

"I'm sorry." His gaze remained on his boot tips.

"It's okay, Tommy. I forgive you." Gabby wiped the last of her tears off her cheeks, then reached her hand out, and he took it. "Let's go pick flowers together."

Walker's chest squeezed at the simple life of children. The apology was accepted so quickly and then Gabby had acted like Tommy hadn't hurt her feelings and made her cry. Walker yearned for their innocent faith.

The kids picked flowers and ran in the field, no hurt feelings. Envy thrummed through Walker. Maybe he could learn something from them.

As Trisha neared the UTV, the sun glinted in his eyes, so he tipped his Stetson lower on his forehead.

After the apology, Gabby hadn't held a grudge against Tommy, which got Walker thinking.

Could he be forgiven for Phoebe's death?

He shook the childlike faith aside. No, it wasn't that

easy. He and everyone who knew him understood Walker was unforgivable.

As Trisha climbed back into the passenger seat, he recalled Sophie's distress yesterday at the birthday party.

"What happened with Sophie during the party?" When he had spotted Trisha walking down the farmhouse front steps, her arm around Sophie, whose chin quivered with emotion and who leaned against her co-guardian like her life depended on it, his heart had squeezed at the young girl's pain.

"She's missing her parents." Trisha frowned. The dusting of freckles across her nose was even more pronounced now with her deep tan.

"The counselor said she'd have days like that and usually they'd be on special days like birthdays or holidays." Sun glinted off Trisha's thick brown hair, turning strands to auburn as the breeze lifted it off her shoulders. He skimmed his fingertips over her shoulder, flicking off a fly. "Thanks for being there for her. For all of them. They couldn't go through this time without you." The children had a mom hole that Trisha filled, except she was never moving to Texas. How was he supposed to raise these children with her in Iowa? Clearly, they needed her here. Maybe she'd change her mind and stay?

"Stop. You're with them all the time. They adore you." Her aquamarine eyes landed on him and jabbed him in the gut. He was so in trouble.

Maybe it was a good thing she lived in Iowa, because she was the first woman he'd been attracted to since Phoebe. Guilt crept up his spine at his wayward attraction. No, he didn't deserve to move on, not after what he had done. He shifted away from her, creating a bit of space between them.

Sophie and Gabby ran toward them, breaking the moment. Each held a fistful of Texas bluebells while Tommy slipped into the seat behind them. "For you," the sisters said in unison.

Trisha slapped a hand to her chest. "Girls, that is so sweet. Thank you." While she collected the pretty flowers, tears edged her eyelashes. She blinked the wetness back. "Get on in." Gabby slid in between them and Trisha draped her arm over the girl. Her fingertips grazed his shirt for a moment.

He started the UTV back up, staying slow so everyone could see the property.

They continued their trek, turning into a lightly wooded area. The dappled shade from the trees felt refreshing against the scorching late-June sun.

"Walka, a steam." Gabby pointed at the running water.

"Can we stop?" Sophie asked.

"For my princess, anything." He pulled under the shade of a tree and parked. After he set the parking brake, turned off the ignition and pocketed the key, he joined the others scrambling to take off their boots and socks so they could wade in the stream.

A smile tipped his lips at the change in plans. Instead of driving and seeing, they had stopped to experience things. Life was not about lists or accomplishing tasks, he realized, but about spending time with people he loved. Trisha was right—there was more to guardianship than providing a secure home for the children. He loved them and wanted to create memories with them.

Once barefoot, he helped the kids over the slippery rocks and into the gurgling water.

Trisha turned to him, a wide grin playing across her lips. Lips he should not be looking at, though he couldn't deny the emotion swirling in his chest at her close proximity.

He put his hand out to help her over the moss-covered rocks. On her first step, she slipped and fell into him, but he caught her and helped steady her. She thanked him and moved on, but the smoky look she'd given him left him wanting to hold her longer. Was he only imagining the affection in her eyes?

As he shook the hopeful thought away, a scream pierced the air. He turned to see Gabby had fallen into the water and was on all fours, sobbing. His pulse quickened at his custodial inadequacy. Trisha rushed to the girl, but Walker could already see blood washing into the stream.

He hurried to help, but by the time he got to their side, Trisha had whipped her fanny pack around and dug out a paper towel to hold to the wound. She tenderly palmed Gabby's cheek as she consoled the little girl.

"Up, up," Gabby tearfully said as he neared. He lifted the girl into his arms as Trisha wrapped a bandage on the wound. Gabby must have seen the wetness in his eyes, because she rubbed her fingers along his scruffy cheek. "I okay, Walka." He swallowed the lump in his throat.

"We should head back," Trisha stated, which only made Tommy and Sophie grumble and complain.

Trisha shot them a look before they turned and obediently headed for the utility terrain vehicle.

Walker trailed behind the pack. Unease slid through him as the gravity of being responsible for these children hit him square between the eyes.

What had Parker and Avery been thinking?

Trisha should have gotten custody of them. They'd be better off with her.

Chapter Six

A wave of panic thundered in Walker's chest as he walked into his mother's kitchen on Saturday afternoon. Memories of Phoebe tilling soil in his mother's garden ran through his mind on a loop. He hadn't visited the garden, one of Phoebe's favorite places, since the accident. And because of him, she wasn't here today.

He plunked the bucket of hand-picked vegetables down and gripped the edges of the cold counter. Why had Parker and Avery chosen him to raise their children? He was a colossal failure at keeping loved ones safe.

The notion of his mother helping those sweet children make pasta primavera in this very kitchen, just like she and Phoebe had done numerous times, battered his heart. The blow of memories charged back, bringing along fresh pain.

With his feet rooted on the faded linoleum, he tried to shake off the image, but it was too deeply embedded— as though a bright red neon sign flashed *All your fault*.

"Remembering Phoebe?" Autumn interrupted as she plopped onto a bar stool and slid the novel she'd been reading onto the green speckled laminate.

He released his grip on the counter and took in his sister. She'd come back from a stint in Dallas right around the time Phoebe had died. Seemed she had been hiding something about her time away, so for that reason, Walker felt he could trust her.

"Kind of." Chicken. How come it was so hard to be honest about his feelings concerning the accident?

Autumn leaned forward, poured a glass of sweet tea from the sweating pitcher on the counter and eyed him. "What's going on with you and Trisha?"

"Nothing," he barked. "We're just friends. It's easier that way, and I don't have to worry about..."

"Getting hurt."

"No! That's not it." He gulped in fresh air and tried to calm down. Why was his sister bringing his baggage into the kitchen? "We are caring for the kids together. End of story." The hair on the back of his neck lifted at his evasiveness.

Autumn didn't understand that he couldn't justify being close to a woman as genuine and loving as Trisha. He hadn't earned it and certainly didn't deserve it.

She stared at him. He shifted. How come she could see through him like no one else?

"Still punishing yourself?" she stated more than asked.

"What?"

"The accident that wasn't your fault."

"You don't understand." The blame pressing against his shoulders felt like it had increased tenfold.

"I do. More than you'll ever know." She rested her chin on her interlaced fingers. "It's time to stop. Move on."

"I've moved on."

"No, you haven't. You're longing for forgiveness." She speared him with a look.

"I don't deserve it."

"That's the point." Autumn leaned forward. "None of us do."

She was right—he had to return to living. Fully be there for the people he loved, especially the children. The only way he could do that was to relinquish his heavy burden. But how?

"The accident was the other driver's fault," she reminded him. "Not yours. Don't beat yourself up over this forever."

"I know." He did. He really did. But forgiving himself seemed impossible.

Phoebe would never take another breath. Celebrate another birthday. She'd never have that child they'd dreamed of. All because of him.

He gazed out the window, across the pasture dotted with Angus cattle. He'd loved Phoebe—that much he'd gotten right. But he hadn't been able to save her.

Stop. The accident wasn't your fault. His breathing evened out as he forced what the police and Phoebe's parents had told him to sink in and take hold.

"God forgave us first," Autumn stated. "If you don't forgive yourself, you're belittling God's work on the cross."

His stomach bottomed out. She was right, wasn't she? Tears formed at the backs of his eyes, but he fought them and won. He was demeaning his faith by carrying this heavy load all by himself. God didn't want that; in fact, God offered him rest.

Yet Walker couldn't help but still feel responsible. He swiveled, grabbed the bucket and again turned to the window so she couldn't read his face. He plucked the tomatoes from the array of vegetables and spread them on the windowsill.

The car accident and Phoebe's passing hadn't taken God by surprise.

God didn't want him living in the past, especially raising these three sweet children.

Could he truly be forgiven and move on? Nah, it couldn't be that easy.

"So, how's the horse farm coming?" Autumn interrupted his pondering. The ice clinked in her glass as she shook the amber liquid around.

"Tight. Parker and Avery had known it would be a challenge, and they were right." He dragged a hand across his chin. "I'm kind of thankful for the housing developer, because I know we have an escape hatch."

"Don't talk like that. It'll work out."

He glanced out the window as Trisha threw her head back and laughed. Before he knew it, emotion bubbled up in him. Whether he liked it or not, he cared about her.

The sun glinted off her long auburn hair. Did she know how gorgeous she was?

No. She didn't. In fact, she didn't seem to understand her worth, not just her good looks, but her intellect, even the way she comforted each child with soft words.

But Walker wasn't about to head down that path again. He had loved Phoebe and lost her, shattering his heart. He never wanted to walk through that gut-wrenching pain again.

"What are you smiling about?" Autumn cocked her head.

He glanced away from the side window, but not fast enough.

"You know," Autumn said as she grinned like a Cheshire cat, "I've seen how you and Trisha look at each other. There's more there than merely caring for the children."

"Wait. You think Trisha likes me?"

Autumn rolled her eyes. "Of course she does."

Maybe his sister was right. If so, what then?

They both valued God and family. When they were together, he felt like a better person. Was it because of Trisha?

A very real part of him wanted to find out if there could be a future with her. He wanted to test the waters and take a chance with Trisha. While that excited him a little, mostly it scared him to death. It all came back to how much he didn't deserve a second chance. Not with Phoebe gone.

"It doesn't matter because she's going back to Iowa," he stated. "Did you know she got a promotion at the end of the school year?" No way was she going to stay here with her career on the upswing.

"How do you know?"

"Google."

"You've been googling her? Man, you have it bad." She grabbed her book and returned to the couch.

Autumn was right—he had it bad. He didn't want to, but he did.

His feelings for Trisha had become stronger with each passing day, and he couldn't do a single thing about his rising emotions.

He snagged a paper towel and wiped out the vegetable bowl, then stole another look out the side window. His heart stuttered at the sight of her.

"It's time you started living again, Walker."

He glared at his nosy sister now lounging on the couch and stomped out of the kitchen. She couldn't comprehend the loss he'd been through.

As he reached for the side door, his steps faltered. It

might not make sense to others, but there was no way he could allow himself to fully enjoy life when he was here and Phoebe wasn't.

That was the price he paid for being alive when she no longer was.

Later that day, excitement bubbled within Trisha as she helped Tommy into his saddle. The boy perched in the seat and clutched the saddle horn for all he was worth. "Hold the reins like we talked about, sweetie, remember?" He grasped the reins in his left hand and the horn in his right. "Good job, buddy." Only he and Walker were riding with Western gear today. She and the girls were riding English style. Part of her hoped the girls might one day want to compete in shows, like she had as a teen.

The moment of slipping and falling into Walker's sturdy chest the other day plagued her. Her fingertips had brushed his soft chambray shirt, and she'd been close enough to inhale a spicy scent around his neck. But the most memorable note had been when she'd looked up into his yummy chocolate eyes and interest had shimmered in their depths. She had jerked her hands away and scurried into the water after the children.

She wasn't falling for him, was she? No. She'd been burned before and she'd not allow someone close enough to hurt her again. Her focus was on the children, her sole purpose for being here this summer.

Sophie, on Gypsy, and Tommy, on Treasure, turned in their seats and waited at the mouth of the pasture trail for the rest of their group. Walker settled Gabby in front of him on the saddle and wrapped his left arm around the girl. She tipped her head against his muscular chest and smiled. Behind him were the worn saddlebags he'd borrowed from his father with their picnic lunch inside, but his face held concern. Was he still worried about Gabby's minor scratch? No, with his forehead and brows furrowed that deeply, something more serious than the girl's minor fall was bothering him. But what?

After Trisha mounted her mare, she joined the group, tipping her cowboy hat forward to shade the sun. "How about you lead, since you've been on the property the most? I'll bring up the rear." He clucked and his gelding moved forward. They made a haphazard line as they walked down the path separating the pastures.

Trisha tried not to admire the way he looked in the saddle, especially holding on to little Gabby.

When Walker threw her a grin over his shoulder, her heart flip-flopped. He was the kind of handsome you'd see modeling swanky Western gear, but it was obvious he didn't understand how attractive he was.

Soon, a peaceful lake flanked by a peeling structure came into view.

"We're here." He stopped at the hitching post, off to the side of the gazebo sorely in need of a paint job.

"What a gorgeous setting." Trisha slid off her horse, took Gabby from Walker and put the squealing four-year-old on the ground. Her fingers grazed Walker's with the handoff and warmth unfurled in her chest at the light touch.

Like a pro, Sophie swung her foot over Gypsy and Tommy wiggled down from Treasure. While Walker tied all the horses to the shaded hitching post, the kids kicked their boots off and started running around the wide-open field, their laughter filling the air.

When Gabby had fallen in the stream, Walker's anxious response had warmed Trisha's heart. It was heart-warming to see a grown man cry at a child's tiny scratch.

Walker took the food out of his gelding's saddlebags while Trisha shimmied free of the backpack picnic blanket Cora had loaned her. In the distance, Texas bluebells bloomed, painting the ground with a variety of purple shades.

"Mrs. Johnson stopped by right before we left," Walker stated. "They are moving to North Carolina and will no longer be leasing Blaze."

Trisha sucked in a breath. So that was the reason for his pinched expression earlier. "Oh no." Most customers shared leased horses, but the Johnsons exclusively leased Blaze. This was a big hit.

"We have to figure a way out of this hole." He glared at her as though she were personally responsible for the Johnsons' move out of state.

"I know," she snapped. His head jerked back as though she'd slapped him. "I'm sorry. It's just that the stakes are so high." She gazed at the happy children, who had no idea their future was so uncertain.

"Hopefully the flyers you posted, advertising boarding and horses for lease, will create some foot traffic soon."

She gave him an appreciative glance for understanding the pressure she was under with the horse farm. Surely, he felt the same.

"Listen, Trisha. I can't thank you enough for stepping up and taking over as barn manager."

"I'm really enjoying myself."

"I almost forgot—how did your call go with Lauren?"

"Good." She had tried to put the distressing call with the college student out of her mind. Being unable to meet with Lauren in her cozy campus office had made Trisha feel like a failure. "We figured out her issues and made a solid plan," she said with a forced lift in her voice. Lauren had needed her there. In person. But Trisha couldn't be in two places at once.

"I'm glad to hear that," he said. "You know, having you run the barn is making this business personal to the boarders, and that's key. Creating community and a personal touch is essential to keeping customers." His belief in her shone as bright as the sun.

Because she'd grown up with such insecurity, she cherished the praise. She had never felt good enough, especially when Foster's parents had yanked away their job offer when he had dumped her. They made her doubt herself, but Foster's parents had been so wrong. Her confidence swelled at her current success in the barn manager role.

"Thanks for that. Now, help me with the blanket," she said to get the focus off her. Next to the gazebo, she opened the blanket, and Walker helped her settle it on the ground, anchoring the corners with the children's boots.

They made a great team. She would miss this when she returned to her predictable life in Iowa. Off to the campus every day at eight. A packed turkey-and-cheese sandwich, chips and an apple for lunch. A frozen meal for dinner, along with a couple of game shows before turning in for the night to read a few chapters of a romance novel. She'd been happy. But after two weeks here, her old life no longer held the same allure, although she seriously missed her students.

"It's great to see the children happy and playing on the land their parents desired them to be raised."

"Agreed. I just hope they can keep living here." The concern in his voice about their predicament settled between them. He shifted his Stetson, leaving most of his face in the shade, and cleared his throat. "All in all, I think they are doing well."

Tommy rushed over. "I'm thirsty."

"Can we eat?" Gabby whined.

They settled on the blanket and Trisha doled out the food. "The prior owners built the gazebo and hitching post—did y'all know that?" She gazed into their trusting faces. "Apparently, when their kids were little, they'd wanted a special place on the farm where they could come and just relax as a family."

Sophie straightened. "That's what we're doing."

"Yes, we are. In fact, their daughter's husband proposed in that very gazebo. Isn't that romantic?" She took in the small peeling structure. She could imagine a fresh coat of paint and twinkle lights creating a romantic sunset proposal. A handsome man kneeling in front of her with a jewelry box open, a sparkling ring nestled inside.

No. That would never happen to her. For starters, tying herself to a man and a potential heartbreak was not a dream but a nightmare scenario.

Sophie tilted her head. "I love that story." Her voice sounded more like a lovesick teenager's than a seven-year-old's. Trisha was absolutely not looking forward to the teenage years and dating.

"Can somebody bless the food so we can eat?" Tommy mumbled.

"Lord," Walker started, "thank You for the day, for this gorgeous setting and for the memories we are making. Lord, we also thank You for Trisha's willingness to come here from Iowa and make our new house a home, and for the blessing she is to our little tribe. Amen."

Trisha's throat tightened at the kind words. She had never considered herself a blessing to anyone.

Undeserving. Forgettable. Never enough. But certainly never a blessing.

Absently, she twisted her college ring. Had she been wrong all this time? Was she worthy enough to have a happily-ever-after?

She peeked at Walker to find him staring at her. He winked and then grabbed a handful of pretzels.

Her heart dropped. If Walker kept up his kind words, this cowboy might just steal her heart, and that was the very last thing she wanted this summer.

Right then, her phone dinged an incoming text message. It was from Buck, informing her that Riptide had colic. It had come on suddenly and Buck had tried everything, but the horse wasn't getting better. Trisha sucked in a breath.

"What's wrong?" Walker put his food down and leaned forward.

"We've gotta go. Sorry, kids." Trisha hurriedly gathered their lunch makings as she explained the severity of the problem to Walker.

Please, God, heal Riptide. We can't afford to lose a valuable horse or pay for emergency surgery.

Though she knew God heard her, she couldn't help but worry about the horse and the ongoing tight financial situation Serenity Stables was in.

Chapter Seven

As soon as they arrived back at the barn, Trisha rushed off and Amanda helped Walker with the children and stabling the horses. While he removed the tack, his rebellious mind turned back to the split second almost a week ago when Trisha had fallen into him at the creek. Had she really hung on to his hand for an extra moment, or had it been his imagination?

Oh, man, his attraction to Trisha was growing stronger, just like his sister had intimated, but he had to keep pushing the feelings away. He didn't have a choice. He'd sworn to never love again because he knew he would fail at protecting her, and he wasn't sure he could go through that heartbreak again.

As Wilbur shuffled over, he shook away the unwelcome thoughts. "I can take the kids back to my place while you focus on Riptide," the older man stated, worry lacing his eyes.

Walker straightened. Was colic that serious? Must be. He agreed, and as Wilbur took the giggling kids toward his modest home, Walker joined the contingent hovering outside the horse's stall. The urgency of everyone's stances sent a chill rippling down his spine.

"Did someone call Earl?" Trisha asked from where she stood in the stall corner, her distraught gaze locked with the gelding's as though willing him to get better.

"I did," Buck stated. "He'll be here as soon as he can."

Trisha gave a quick nod, but the fun picnic atmosphere had turned dire. Though Walker had grown up with cattle and a few horses, he didn't remember a time where a horse was in jeopardy like this.

Riptide turned his attention from Trisha's soothing voice to bite at his side. Then he lifted his back leg and kicked at his belly a few times before letting out an exasperated breath.

"Has he been doing this for a while?" Trisha asked.

"I just finished cleaning the stalls and noticed he hasn't passed manure all day," Buck said. "When I came back to check on him, he was rolling."

Trisha gave him a sharp look.

"I know. That's when I texted you. He never rolls."

"Never," Trisha muttered as she let herself out of the stall. "Have you been walking him?"

Buck lifted the lead in his hand. "Every fifteen minutes. I was just about to walk him around the building again. Want me to?"

"Yes, thank you, Buck." She gave him a nod of appreciation and stood back as he guided the gelding down the aisle. Every few steps, the horse either stopped to chew at his side or kick a back foot into his stomach.

"What's happening?"

"It's colic, which is basically a stomach or intestinal issue, like blockages or twists." Trisha's focus clung to Riptide until they turned the corner. Then she flashed her anguished gaze to Walker. What he saw in her eyes downright scared him. "Horses can't throw up, so they have to work everything through their system."

"How'd it happen?"

"I'm not sure. Colic can come on from food changes, too much exercise, even stress, or being cooped up too much. But since we just switched grain manufacturers, I'm guessing it's from his new food." She wrapped her arms around herself. "His discomfort is just ripping me up inside."

"He'll be okay, right?"

She slid him a side-glance. "Usually colic resolves itself in twelve to twenty-four hours."

"I hear Riptide isn't himself," the vet said as he rushed into the barn. Earl placed a large bag inside the stall.

Trisha gave him the details while Buck returned and stabled the horse.

Walker, Trisha and Buck circled the wooden door as Earl pressed a stethoscope against the gelding's stomach.

"He's listening for gut sounds," Trisha whispered.

Soon, he began checking Riptide's vitals. The concerned expression on Earl's face worried Walker.

"He's in a lot of pain, so I'm going to give him some Banamine," Earl said as he put a syringe into the horse's mouth for a moment. "I'll use the stomach tube to get mineral oil in his stomach." He then coaxed Riptide to swallow the end of a tube and seemed to snake it through his system.

The gelding fought back by shaking his head, but at least he was focused on something positive now.

Trisha clasped Walker's upper arm and squeezed. "Let's hope the mineral oil gets things moving."

As Walker patted her petite hand, he noted her anxiety

had dulled since Earl had come on the scene. For now, he'd take his cues from her and stop making such a big fuss over the gelding. Surely, the vet would fix the horse.

He dragged his hand away from hers. The pull toward her was real, but opening himself up to someone again petrified him. She deserved better than him, but since she didn't see his obvious defect, he himself would have to protect her from him. He didn't have a choice.

Once Trisha learned the mistakes of his past, she'd look at him differently and she would absolutely not smile and reach her hand out to him.

Soon, Earl pulled the tube out and Trisha audibly sighed. "We'll see if those mineral oils in his tummy will do the trick." He packed up his things. "If he needs it, I'll be back around five to give him another session of medication and oil. In the meantime, walk him, no food, small amounts of warm water only." He nodded and left the barn.

"Buck, why don't you get back to work and I'll handle this?" Trisha asked as she clipped the lead on the gelding.

Buck tipped his hat at her and lumbered to the lower barn.

Walker walked with her as Riptide kept stopping to chew his side or kick a back foot into his stomach. All Walker could think to do was pray. So he did.

"While there isn't a lesson, let's walk him in the ring," Trisha said, then turned.

A while later, they returned to his stall and she asked Walker to go to the house for warm water. The unease on her face spoke volumes, so he was afraid to ask what she thought the horse's prognosis was.

At the house, he filled a small thermos with warm

water and returned to the barn to find Trisha pacing in the corner of the stall. She twirled at his appearance.

"What if he doesn't make it?" Her face squished up in agitation.

He pulled her into a hug. "He'll be fine," Walker stated, though he hadn't realized the situation was so grim.

Trisha hovered while offering the horse warm water, which he refused.

"Hey, guys." Autumn appeared at Riptide's stall. "How's he doing?"

"No change," Trisha responded in a tight voice that shook Walker to the core.

"How about I get the kids from Wilbur?" she asked. "I picked up a pizza and ice cream. I was thinking I could let them watch a movie while they ate and then I'll put them to bed."

"That would be awesome," Walker said to his sister as he gave her a grateful look.

Shortly, Earl arrived to do another session of medication and oil. This time his face appeared tighter, which made Walker even more concerned.

After the veterinarian departed, Buck and Ryder checked in and then left for the day while he and Trisha kept walking the horse and offering him warm water, which he continued to refuse.

"We should put him in the trailer and drive up and down the gravel road," Trisha said, her face eager. "The motion might jostle Riptide's insides and maybe help him loosen a blockage or break up gas bubbles into smaller bits so that it can pass through."

Her excitement infused him with hope. "Sure, I'll hook up the trailer," he said as he rushed off.

"I can't believe I forgot about that," she called after

him. "I've had great success doing it in the past with other horses."

Once the trailer was connected, they loaded Riptide, who continued to bite at his side and lift his back leg to kick at his belly. Walker wasn't sure if the horse was still distressed or if it had become a new habit. They settled in the truck's cab with their windows down and started driving. He made a point to stay on gravel or bumpy pavement.

Trisha looked at the glowing digital clock on the dashboard. Somehow, it had gotten dark. "We need to be back for Earl in an hour," she said, gravel kicking up under the tires as she spoke.

"The kids really enjoyed the picnic today." She broke the nighttime silence, obviously trying to get her mind off the horse. "They appreciate your mother, and being part of the Wednesday night family dinners and sitting in the family pew at church. Those things make me feel special too."

Walker steered around a pothole. They weren't looking to make Riptide more uncomfortable. "You are family, always will be," he stated, knowing their tie with the orphaned children would last a lifetime.

"You are so sweet." She touched her index finger to the corners of her eyes, as though to stop any errant tears from falling. "Your parents don't know how their kindness touches me."

Oh, he knew. She'd told him that his parents had been the mom and dad she'd always dreamed of. He heard a stomp and glanced at Trisha, who grimaced back. Didn't sound like the bumpy ride was helping the horse.

"It's almost time for Earl to come for another round of medication and oil."

He turned the rig around and headed back to the farm, the gravel in the road kicking up as he drove. "It's been hours. Shouldn't Riptide be getting better?" His throat clenched at the seriousness of the situation.

Even in the darkness, he spotted her nibbling her lower lip. "Colic requires time and patience. Let's just pray it doesn't turn into a surgery."

Surgery? The thought hollowed his stomach. He knew they might be at risk of losing the horse farm. Apparently, that reality was becoming much more real with each passing moment.

The following evening, Trisha put the girls to bed and left their room, exhausted by everything she'd done to help Riptide, yet the gelding wasn't getting any better.

She opened the screen door and faltered when she spotted Walker on the wide porch swing, the only item in sight to sit on. "Where are the rockers?"

"Archie has them. I helped him load them into his truck earlier so he could clean and restain them. I guess he does it every couple of years." He patted the ample space beside him as though sitting so close to him wouldn't ratchet up her heart rate.

She gulped. Her gaze flitted to the generous steps she could sit on, but since she didn't want to offend him, she settled on the swing and huddled against the wooden arm.

"Earl called me on my way down the stairs. He wants everyone to stay away for about an hour because he's thinking Riptide might be nervous with everyone watching him," she said. The ceiling fans above slowly whirred, giving them a slight breeze in the still and sticky night.

Something about Walker's presence calmed her. Why?

Attractive men usually made her nervous, but a strange combination of tranquility and pleasure seeped into her being when around Walker. She drank in the comfort of his nearness while her unease over Riptide ran deep.

"He called me too." Walker's concerned features likely mirrored hers. "I'm trusting in God and Earl. We have so many people praying for Riptide."

She peeked at him. Boy, he was drop-dead gorgeous. Yes, he was good-looking with a cowboy hat on, but in the evenings after he cleaned up, with his wavy hair slightly damp and parted just so, he looked *GQ* handsome.

"You've been around colic horses many times. Yesterday, you told me Riptide would be better in twenty-four hours," he said as he stroked his fingers over his clean-shaven jaw. "It's been going on a lot longer, closing in on thirty-six." The worry on his face spoke volumes.

"Earl's doing everything he can." Her words sounded comforting, but deep inside, she'd grown overly concerned for Riptide. Earl was an amazing vet, but he'd tried everything multiple times and the horse was only getting worse.

"What'll happen if Earl can't fix him?"

Trisha lifted her face to the vast sky. "Surgery. Which is expensive and not always successful." A tear leaked out, and she knuckled it away.

"Hey, Riptide will be okay," Walker stated as he rubbed her knee for a moment. Then his hand snapped away like he'd been touching a burning fire. He shifted a little, as though embarrassed, and created a bit more space between them on the swing.

Not for the first time, she considered what would happen when she returned to Iowa. The kids appeared to rely on having her around, and the five of them had a good schedule. She glanced at Walker, who was now gazing up at the endless sky filled with stars and a sliver of a moon. Three weeks and *this* felt like home to her, way more than her life in Iowa. But after Labor Day she was leaving, so she couldn't allow herself to become too comfortable.

"Your mom texted she was praying," she said.

"I'm not surprised."

"You know, I never really had a family. But yours has always opened their home to me." During her summers in college, Wade had not only taught her to rope calves, but had also given her business advice through the years. Cora had taught her the life skill of cooking, and also made time for Trisha whenever something was on her mind.

"I'm glad." He looked over, and their eyes met. At his attention, her pulse notched higher. His chocolate eyes had little flecks of gold in them. How had she never noticed that? She dragged her gaze away.

During freshman year, she, Foster, Parker, Avery, Walker and Phoebe had become friends. Three couples who had done everything together. They'd remained tight during their college years and Trisha had relished the family feel of the gang. She had treasured each of them. When Foster had dumped her and dropped out of the group, the rest had huddled around Trisha in support.

Then Phoebe died and it almost felt like they'd lost Walker. But in time, he'd reemerged, and somehow the remaining group had stayed close. "That's why losing Avery and Parker was so hard on me," she continued. "But feeling like part of your family helps me so much. I mean, Cora and Wade treat me like one of theirs, and this summer has reminded me how much that relationship means to me."

"They love you," he said, then shifted uncomfortably as though he wished he could snatch those words back.

She recalled the recent fun morning in Cora's garden, and how agitated Walker had appeared until he'd finally stalked into the house. But when he had returned from the kitchen, an empty vegetable bowl in hand, he'd been visibly at peace.

"The other day, at your mother's garden, you seemed upset." She told herself it was a coguardian concern, not romantic. At all.

He stilled, then licked his lips before answering. "The car accident."

Surely, he didn't still consider himself responsible for the accident that had taken his wife's life? Not after the police had completely cleared him and Phoebe's family had agreed it wasn't Walker's fault.

"I feel like I could have reacted quicker. Done more." His gaze drifted into the night. "So there wasn't a fatality," he whispered.

Except, they'd been T-boned by a drunk driver without headlights on. No one could have reacted in time. No one.

"I feel like I made some headway talking with Autumn in my mother's kitchen."

He explained what he and his sister had discussed.

As Walker talked, Trisha listened. It felt good to concentrate on something other than Riptide's painful colic. She knew Walker didn't share this story with many people, so she felt fortunate he trusted her enough to share.

When he got to the details of that night, his jaw shifted. He said nothing for a moment and then a sheen of moisture glazed his eyes.

Her heart squeezed with empathy for him and she

whispered a silent prayer that someday he could forgive himself.

As an ache pressed in on her chest, she covered his hand with her own. He'd been carrying this pain for years.

"Thanks." He slid her a sideways smile that made her pulse jump. "I feel better talking with you about it." Then he gave her one of his big grins.

Her heart danced a jig that Walker had shared such a momentous moment with her.

She bumped his shoulder. "See, Autumn was a big help."

He pursed his lips, again staring into the dark night. "You're right." His gaze sharpened on her and something sizzled between them.

What she saw in his eyes took her breath away. Something had shifted between them, and she wasn't sure what it was.

She popped to her feet. He didn't like her, did he? She fretted her hands and paced the porch.

"What's wrong?" He came up beside her and she practically leaped off the porch.

"Nothing. I mean, I'm exhausted." Their eyes locked for a moment, and she saw it again. She didn't want to consider how their relationship seemed to develop deeper with every passing day.

Could they work?

Was there even a *them*? Her mind traveled to the look he'd given her tonight. Twice. She gulped.

No. Romance would throw their nice, neat coguardianship into a blender, and she couldn't have that.

The children deserved more. They deserved stability, which a nonromantic relationship between them would provide.

And that was a good thing, because when she was in a relationship and allowed herself to get too involved, it gave far too much control to someone else. She never wanted that to happen again.

Regardless, after Foster had broken off their engagement, something in her had stopped believing in happily-ever-after.

Her phone dinged.

An urgent message from Earl to come to Riptide's stall. They rushed to the lower barn.

"I'm sorry, but I've done everything I can. Riptide needs emergency surgery."

Her gaze collided with Walker's and they nodded, silently agreeing on the surgery. Yes, they wanted Riptide to heal and be healthy, but the bill would be thousands of dollars they didn't have on an already narrow budget.

She decided now was not the right time to tell Walker just how much the surgery would cost.

He'd been staring at charts and graphs since day one, like a pressure cooker getting ready to erupt. Things had been a struggle from the start, and this surgery expense just might be the tipping point for Walker to announce it was time to take Silver Developers up on its offer.

Please, God, don't let this one event take the horse farm from the children.

But as she finished her prayer, she knew the chances were slim they'd be able to keep the farm.

Chapter Eight

A warm breeze drifted through the open window, bringing in the pleasant smell of fresh-cut grass. A week had
passed since something had shifted in his relationship
with Trisha. Walker wasn't sure what had happened that
evening on the front porch, but the past week had been
beyond awkward as they both attempted to adjust to fo-
cusing on the kids and the barn and ignoring their growing attraction. At least, Walker assumed the feelings were
mutual.

His chair squeaked as he leaned back and took in Wilbur, who had been coming in to Walker's barn office to
chat most days. Many times with interesting tidbits of
information about Serenity Stables that he didn't know.

"Glad Riptide handled the surgery so well," Wilbur
said as he scratched Lilly Bug's ears. Whenever the older
man sat, the terrier jumped in his lap as though to claim
him.

"Yes, with flying colors." While Walker was grateful for the successful outcome, that surgery was going
to cost them a lot, though he hadn't yet received the bill.

Wilbur nodded and continued. "Now, I've been thinking of ways to increase the bottom line. There are two fields that Archie just mows flat every fall because we don't need that much hay." Wilbur shifted Lilly Bug on his lap. "Either bale and sell it or let the feed store know that someone can come and bale the hay themselves." He lowered his chin and looked at Walker over the top of his glasses. "For a price, of course."

Walker straightened. "Really?" At the idea of passive income, an adrenaline rush hit his veins as though he'd just chugged a cup of strong coffee. "I'll have to discuss this with Archie."

He thanked Wilbur and then invited him to Sunday lunches at the Triple C. His mother had been nagging him to, though Walker wasn't sure what his reticence had been, because the older man now felt like family.

Wilbur stood and Lilly Bug jumped to the ground. "Thanks for the invite," he said as he rubbed his stomach. "I've heard about your mother's cooking and I'd love to join y'all." He made to leave and then turned around. "Skeeter and Riley Girl are expecting babies again. I'd love to save three puppies so each of the kids could have one."

The mention of more work dimmed Walker's excitement over the hay fields. "We have enough on our plate, but thanks for thinking of the kids." Walker couldn't handle one more thing right now. He felt like he was drowning as it was.

As Wilbur ambled out of the office, he stopped to gather fresh carrots to feed the horses on his way. The place hummed with activity, unlike before Trisha had arrived. She'd gotten more leasers and more boarders; maybe they could make this place a success before she left in September. Walker lifted his hand in welcome to one of the teenage boarders and her mopey brother as they passed.

Walker texted Archie to drop by when he had a minute. He couldn't wait to talk over the idea about letting another farmer come onto their fields to bale up hay. How much could he reasonably charge?

Trisha and her brunette locks passed in a flash. A smile tipped his lips and his feet automatically found purchase, as though a magnet attracted them. The old office chair groaned as he stood. Maybe she needed a hand. No, he wasn't aiming to spend more time with her—he was simply trying to help.

Trisha had one of their boarded horses on a lead, guiding the mount toward the pasture.

"Want me to bring anyone?" he called.

She turned, a bright smile on her face. "Sure. Grab Scout."

He clipped a lead on Scout's halter and followed Trisha. After he unclipped the lead, the quarter horse took off to join the other horses in the far corner of the pasture.

Trisha closed the old metal gate, shimmied the lock in place and leaned against the railing, focused on the group of horses. The wind whipped through her long locks and she pushed a section away from her mouth. Did she know how naturally pretty she was?

Lilly Bug and Dip Dip raced over as though they were missing something and jumped at his boots. The Jack Russells no longer bothered him. In fact, he couldn't imagine the horse farm without them around.

"I've been experimenting with a rate increase every year over the next five." He propped his boot on the rail. "I was thinking we could go slow so we don't lose customers, but it'll get us to the competitive rate we should be at right now." He tugged on the brim of his hat to shade his eyes from the sun and then also told her about Wilbur's hay idea.

"What great ideas, Walker." The approval on her face shone and made him feel all warm inside. She held her fist out and he bumped her knuckles.

The momentary physical contact made his pulse jump.

"Do you feel confident about being able to keep the farm?" Her gaze landed on him and unspoken emotions flickered in the gorgeous emerald depths.

"With the slow price increases and the passive hay income, let's just say I'm more optimistic."

"Well, I got the bill for Riptide's surgery," she said as her lips tightened into a thin line.

When she told him the amount, his head reeled. He'd expected a large bill, but not that gigantic.

To steady himself, he put his boots on level ground. "You know what this means, don't you?"

"We'll work something out, Walker. We have to. The kids can't lose this place and I refuse to sell to a housing developer." She pushed off from the fence and stalked back to the upper barn, where she'd successfully placed all the boarded and leased horses. She'd been right— making that move had made those riders create a tighter organic community.

Except, ignoring their dire financial situation wouldn't make it go away.

Riptide's emergency surgery bill had put them over the edge. They might as well call Silver Developers today, because there was no way out of this mess. He and Trisha had tried, but they'd failed.

He trailed after her. Lilly Bug and Dip Dip bolted past him. As soon as she stepped foot in the barn, a boarder had her in deep conversation about which horse shows to compete in this season.

As he walked to the lower barn to help with tacking horses for the midday riding lessons, his boots crunched over the gravel between the barns.

Partway there, he stopped to view the property, surprised at how much pride he took from this place. Six months ago, he'd thought nothing other than cybersecurity would give him such joy, but Serenity Stables had won him over. Unfortunately, their days of trying to make this place a success were about over. After they put the children to bed this evening, he'd have to talk with her about reaching out to Silver Developers. He pushed the ominous thoughts from his head and moved on with his day.

His mind switched gears to earlier when he'd ridden over the property to check for fence failures. He'd listened to a podcast about forgiveness, following up on what he and Autumn had talked about last week. He'd learned that asking God for forgiveness was one step, but he still had to forgive himself.

Could he really forgive himself and learn to move forward?

After batting the idea around all morning, he realized he would need to lay his burden down and let Jesus take it. He kneaded the tight muscles on the back of his neck. He was tired of dragging a boatload of guilt around with him. Walker wanted peace, and he knew he'd never have it until he forgave himself.

How much of life had he missed because he had made decisions from a place of fear?

He nodded. Yes, he was ready. With this peaceful ranch setting surrounding him, he closed his eyes and said a heartfelt prayer, leaving it all at the foot of the cross.

When he opened his eyes, he wiped his tears and grinned because his shoulders felt lighter and the heavy burden he'd been carrying had begun to dissipate.

For the first time in years, the future looked bright. Yes, it was time to leave the past where it belonged and move on with his life.

Maybe even enjoy some happiness if he found it.

While he was on a roll, he decided he'd make another plea. *God, if it be Your will, please save Serenity Stables. Allow Sophie and Tommy and Gabby to live here just like their parents desired. Amen.*

"Walker," Trisha interrupted.

He spun around. "What's up?" Her cheeks were red, her eyes sparkled, and the smile blooming on her face was unstoppable. Her jeans, tucked into her cowgirl boots, were coupled with a black T-shirt, and her long hair trailed over her shoulder.

"You're never going to believe this, but Arielle mentioned that Serenity Stables usually hosts a horse show in mid-July. So I called the Hunter Jumper Circuit coordinator, and sure enough, we're on the schedule."

His stomach dropped at the news. "How much money is this going to cost? Can we get out of it?" The *we should be closing things up and not spending unnecessary money* didn't roll off his tongue like he wanted. She was too excited to knock down. They'd talk later.

"It's worth the investment and, no, we don't want to get out of it."

Befuddled, he trailed after her toward the upper barn, where she snagged paper, pens and water bottles.

"Let's get the kids and take them to your mom's to swim. We can plan the whole thing." She turned and lifted onto her toes in excitement. When she saw his crestfallen expression, she reached for his shoulder. "It'll be okay. I promise."

When her palm left his shirt, he missed it.

His throat clogged with emotion. These feelings for Trisha were stronger than he had thought. Though, once they sold the farm, she'd head back to Iowa, so he wouldn't have to deal with them anymore. That thought saddened him more than it should have.

He grabbed his phone off the charger and helped her corral the kids, with swimsuits, into the truck.

As he nosed the truck down the road, his stomach coiled into a tight knot because the last thing they should do was spend more of the children's money. They needed to get out before it was too late.

Trisha practically vibrated with excitement in the passenger seat.

He swallowed the panic crawling up the back of his throat because he knew he couldn't say no to Trisha. But saying no to this horse show just might be the best financial decision they could make.

Once at the Triple C Ranch, the children rushed around the house to the pool gate while she and Walker unloaded the truck in front of his parents' home. Trisha shoved her phone in her back pocket, willing her hands to stop shaking.

"You okay?" he asked her.

She grabbed the nearest bag so he wouldn't guess how stunned she was at the unexpected news she'd just received. "Of course. Just thinking."

Walker turned his attention to the kids. "Wait for us," he called to them, holding on to his Stetson, as steady as always. He hadn't seemed to notice her shock. Good.

Today he wore a pair of dark-washed jeans with his well-loved boots. His navy blue chambray shirt highlighted his dark eyes every bit as much as his sturdy biceps. How had she never noticed how handsome he was?

The kids danced around the gate and peered over the fence at the enticing water, all three talking at the same time about what pool float they were going to use. As Walker and Trisha reached them, Tommy mentioned doing a cannonball off the diving board.

Walker's jaw stiffened, but he unlocked the gate, told the kids no running and then helped place their things on the chairs scattered around the glass table. Just to make sure her mind wasn't playing tricks on her, she read the surprising text again, then set her phone on the table.

Sophie and Tommy jumped into the pool. Gabby stood in the shallow end, lifting the water with her hands and letting it drain out between her fingers. A smile tilted her lips as she sang a soft song.

The air smelled of mild chlorine mixed with the sunscreen Trisha had liberally applied to the children. Thankfully, her hands were no longer shaking as she pulled towels from the huge pool bag and stacked them on a chair so the kids would see them when they got out.

Maybe after receiving the promotion in the spring, she should have expected the administration to choose her for the elite class she'd always dreamed of teaching at Iowa State. But life had been so hectic these past five months, her mind had been on the kids, not advancing her teaching position.

Seemed her career was truly soaring. Then how come the news about the elite class didn't elate her?

She settled on a swivel deck chair next to Walker's. The shade sail above them sheltered the entire table area and more, which was nice because she spent entirely too much time in the sun at the horse farm and her freckles were out of control. In the distance, goats bleated and chickens clucked; the pool wasn't far from the little petting zoo Cora had set up for the summer camp.

"We won't bother your mother or the summer camp students, will we?"

"Nope. They'll be noisier than us, and for legal reasons, my mom never brings the summer camp kids here." He perched on the edge of his chair, posture stiff. His gaze never wavered from the children.

She knew him well enough to know he wasn't concerned about the welfare of the children, because they knew how to swim, but the financial well-being of the horse farm. After opening the emergency surgery bill, she'd had to agree with him. But they couldn't give up hope.

Gabby had joined her siblings while they splashed and squealed and batted a ball around.

Trisha crammed her phone, and the reminder of her dream class, into her purse. She had thought teaching was what she wanted, but after getting her hands dirty as the barn manager these past weeks, she wondered if maybe staying here might be more fulfilling. The kids would sure like it.

No. Who was she kidding? She had a career in Iowa, one where she was satisfied, and she certainly didn't need to travel down the romance road again. She had made poor choices with men in the past, or at the very least, she couldn't live up to a romantic partner's expectations. Regardless, getting entangled with someone would not be smart, and she wanted to be wise for the kids. The last thing they needed was to have their guardians become romantically involved. They didn't deserve drama in their life, not after everything they'd been through.

Gabby shrieked as Tommy accidentally splashed her. Before Trisha could get up to referee, they worked things out between them.

She gave Walker, who appeared solely focused on the kids, a long look and considered the idea of relocating here. The notion of working as barn manager, instead of as a professor in Iowa, knocked around in her head and wouldn't go away. Would Walker be happy if she stuck around?

Assuming there was even a horse farm to stick around for. She held back a defeated sigh. They could not give up just yet. She had a good feeling this horse show would somehow save the farm, but how?

"I saw you at lunch with the girls," she said.

Earlier today, when he'd played with Sophie and Gabby, he'd had his big hand clasped around a tiny doll. His voice and attitude had been so fun-loving. Her heart raced at the memory of the falsetto voice he had used as he'd wiggled the figurine above the plastic town.

He quirked his brow. "A wise woman once told me to stop and smell the roses. So today I did, by playing with little dolls."

When he looked into her eyes, her pulse sped up. It was one thing to curb her feelings when she knew for sure a man was off the dating circuit for good. It was another thing altogether to resist a man who played dolls with his little girls over his lunch break.

"You know, they're doing pretty well," she stated. "Mostly, they've successfully weathered the storm of losing their parents."

He leaned back. "They are now, but the four months

before you arrived, we had lots of hard days, as you well know." He scratched the stubble lining his jaw. The more time he spent working on the farm, the less he shaved every day, as he had when he'd worked in the computer field. His rough-and-tumble look attracted her.

"I'm not telling you anything you don't already know," he said. "We talked. The kids video chatted with you. They've had a tough road."

Tommy tossed the plastic ball into the floating basketball hoop. When it went in, he whooped.

What if she could stay? Long ago, Trisha had squashed her dream of ever becoming a wife or mother because there was something about her and relationships that had never worked out. If she stayed, they'd be a quasi family, right? No, she had worked hard to get where she was in her career in Iowa.

Walker sighed and leaned back. "Okay, how about I pray to start this planning session." He said a simple prayer, asking God to be at the center of their talk and that the upcoming horse show wouldn't be too overwhelming.

With noises of the children playing and water splashing, Walker tilted his chair to hers. "So, how can this horse show not be a lot of work?"

"We can use everything the prior owners did from last year. Same classes, same format, same forms, same volunteers—all that jazz." She took out the paper and a pen. "Amanda was pretty involved in the past and said she'd pull that information together."

His brow wrinkled. "Really?"

He looked way more tempting when he didn't have those worry lines on his forehead. She focused on the paper in front of her, and not the strong contour of his face.

An errant splash from Tommy's cannonball dampened her paper and she dried it with the edge of a towel.

They discussed the PA system, the course layouts for all the jumper classes, the pros and cons of outside versus indoor ring, and the option of renting bleachers so there'd be more space for spectators. Then she brought up the moneymaker: a tent for not only food but for vendors to sell artwork, saddles, clothes, even construction and tractor sales.

As they talked, he angled closer and closer to her notes, his face perilously near hers.

"I have one more profit idea." She grabbed her phone and flipped to the website of the highly sought after photographer Amanda had shared with her earlier. "We could hire a photographer to take pictures of riders in their classes and the obligatory victory pass. Aren't these pictures stunning?"

He leaned over to look at her phone, cupping the side to cut down on the glare from the sun. "Wow, they sure are." He looked at her and his gaze dropped to her lips and hung there.

She froze. Was he going to kiss her? In front of the kids? Her heart pitter-pattered at the notion.

But as quick as the moment began, it ended when he leaned back in his chair. Seeming nervous.

She released a haggard breath as her heart thudded wildly.

Walker wasn't like any other man she'd dated. He listened when she talked and cared about not just her, but the children and his enormous family.

Did she want him to kiss her? The pounding of her heart said yes, but her head was still way too scared.

She sneaked a glance at Walker. What was happening with him? Did he like her romantically?

Did she *want* him to like her romantically?

Trisha tossed the paper, pen and her phone into her purse and leaned back, relishing the time with these sweet children as her heart rate returned to normal. She enjoyed doing life with Walker. He respected her, she felt safe and accepted with him, and he treated her and the children well. What was not to like about this new life she'd found herself in?

"I hate to dampen the mood, but this," he stated as he waved at her notebook, "will not revive Serenity Stables. I'm sorry, Trisha. This plan looks like it'll break even or make a little money. To dig out of this hole, we need something big or..."

Thankfully, he didn't say what they both were thinking. *It might be time to sell.*

She gave him a nod as her head spun, trying to come up with an idea. One that would get them out of this predicament.

They were at a crossroads and she knew it. What could they do over the course of the show to get them on the right track?

An awesome idea hit, and she straightened. It was pure brilliance. "I know a big name. I can ask him if he'd come and sign stock photos and let people do pictures with him, for a price."

"Who in the world could bring in enough people to pay off that vet bill?"

"Kent Kelton. He's a huge draw because he's been on the Grand Prix jumping circuit for years and he was on the most recent Olympic team where they medaled."

Walker's lips parted and his eyebrows lifted into his hairline. "You know him?"

"Yup. We competed one season together before he

made it big. A group of us are connected on social media and I know his text number."

"So two days of a meet and greet with a huge name?"

She nodded, warmth unfurling in her chest at how pleased he seemed at her idea.

"If we price the meet and greet right, it could very well pay for the emergency surgery." She could practically see the calculator going off in his head.

"Watch me," Sophie called. With a grin on her face, she jumped off the diving board. When she rose to the top, Trisha and Walker clapped. Sophie grinned and paddled to the shallow area to settle in a pink flamingo pool float.

Trisha sent Kent a text, explaining the situation, and hoped he'd be willing to help a charity case.

"If we fail, then we have to sell. That's all there is to it," he said, voice firm. Unfortunately, he was right.

But excitement coursed through her at the possibility of keeping the farm, the children's inheritance and legacy. She glanced at the happy kids and prayed this would somehow work out and they could continue to be raised on the horse farm they'd grown to love.

She couldn't bear to sell their gorgeous farm to a housing developer. Not only would that break five hearts, but they'd fail Parker and Avery's dying wish of their children growing up at Serenity Stables.

Chapter Nine

On the Fourth of July, Trisha trailed after the kids into the pharmacy in downtown Serenity. Patrons filled the usually empty store.

"I can't believe I forgot water bottles," she said as she passed Walker, who held the door open for them. Ever since Kent had replied he was available and eager to participate, they'd both been in higher spirits.

The pharmacy had American stick flags decorating the place. The back wall held a festive red, white and blue Independence Day banner.

"Can we look at the toys?" Sophie wore a charming stars-and-stripes short ensemble, matching Gabby's. Trisha had only talked Tommy into a red shirt, jean shorts and white sneakers. Festive, but not as adorable as what she'd found online that he'd refused to let her purchase.

"As long as the three of you stay together, okay?" Trisha said.

The girl's curls bounced as she gave a solemn nod. She held her siblings' hands and they walked into the crowd of people.

"Got them, but this may take a while," Walker said

as he nodded to the lengthy checkout line, five plastic water bottles sweating in his hands.

She shrugged. "Your family is saving seats, so we aren't in a rush." His arm brushed hers as they moved to the checkout. A rush of goose bumps fanned across her skin, but she beat down her growing emotions yet again.

"When you were lunging Goliath yesterday, I saw you had a saddle on him. Tremendous progress." The way his approving gaze landed on her heated her cheeks.

"I feel like I'm slowly earning his trust." Anyone could have turned the gelding around, because Goliath had great compassion deep inside.

As they moved up a little in line, Walker's phone beeped. He pulled it out. "Awesome. The candidate for barn manager can come in for an interview next week." His thumbs moved across the screen. "Remember this one? He looks perfect on paper. Let's hope we get a good feeling about him in person."

Her vision became wavy at the thought of hiring a barn manager to replace her. The upcoming interview felt like Walker didn't believe in her anymore. Why wasn't he considering that she just might want to stick around longer than the summer?

"Maybe we should wait to see how the horse show goes before hiring someone."

"You're the one who is confident Kent will be a success."

How come the pull to stay on as barn manager was stronger now than the pull to return to her collegiate job— even after receiving the promotion and the elite class she'd just been awarded?

After they purchased the water, they gathered the kids and made their way outside, heading over to the live oak tree and the McCaws, who welcomed them with hugs and loving greetings.

Residents were positioned on both sides of Main Street and countless wore patriotic colors. Many huddled under the live oaks that lined the street to get as much shade as possible on such a sunny summer day. American flags hung from the lampposts. Red, white and blue flowers spilled from flowerpots.

"Now that everyone's here, we have an announcement to make." Ethan, Walker's older brother, got everyone's attention, then gazed into his wife's face. Laney hugged his arm against her side while grinning broadly. "We're going to have a baby!"

A roar rose from the McCaw clan as they all clamored to hug the expectant parents.

True joy lodged deep under Trisha's rib cage. What a delightful family to be part of. As an only child who'd essentially been pushed to the side, these were moments she had always dreamed of, and now, because of Sophie, Tommy and Gabby, she was part of the McCaws.

The more she got to know Walker and his family, the more she wondered if she had been relying on the wrong people all along. She needed to rely solely on God and not on her instincts or what others promised her.

Peace settled over her as Sophie, Tommy and Gabby joined the McCaw children on the curb for a front-row seat.

As the first float rounded the corner of Main Street, the music became louder and she rose onto her toes to see. That slight movement caused her hand to brush Walker's arm. The air around them seemed electrified by the many accidental touches today. From parking the truck, to walking through the booths of games and playing many of them with the kids, to finding their spot among the gaggle of McCaws in the Serenity crowd. It seemed there was a magnet on her hand attracting his attention. She wondered if he was trying to hold her hand and didn't have the guts, or if every touch was simply accidental.

Hearing of Laney's pregnancy sprouted a small seed of yearning in Trisha. After the breakup with Foster, she'd given up on marriage and children, but this summer something inside Trisha had bloomed. Now, more than ever, she wanted a husband one day. Maybe some babies.

These out-of-the-blue thoughts turned her inside out. She'd been content being single, had even felt called to singleness, but now she knew what a healthy relationship felt like. She eyed Walker. Her whole life, she had believed there was something wrong with her, that there was a reason no one would stay with her, yet she wondered if that was just a lie. The McCaws had welcomed her. Loved her. Accepted her. All just as she was. So had Walker.

Her phone buzzed in her pocket. She pulled it out to find an email from Distinguished Professor Spivey. She held in a little yelp. First the elite class and now communication from a DP?

Trisha, I hope this email finds you well. I have a paper I planned to present at the Kentucky Equine Research Conference, but alas, I'm unable to attend. Since you assisted me with the initial research last summer, I was hoping you could present for me.

Squeak. Yes, she'd love to. Was honored he'd thought of her.

She scanned the message again and noticed the presentation date was the same weekend of the horse show.

Her throat tightened. She shoved her phone into her pocket. A part of her shriveled at the thought of saying no to this huge request.

Walker snagged her gaze and lifted his brows in question. She shook her head that it was nothing to be concerned with.

What had she been thinking earlier about staying here as barn manager? She'd be crazy to walk away with Lauren needing her, all the other students she mentored, her recent promotion, the elite class, and now DP Spivey asking for help. Her career in Iowa was soaring.

The marching band came closer, horns blaring and drums beating. Sophie got up and wove through the crowd toward Trisha, unshed tears threatening. Trisha's stomach twisted at the distressing look in the girl's eyes as she wrapped her hand around Trisha's wrist and tugged.

Trisha crouched low to face the seven-year-old. "Is everything okay?"

"My parents were here last year for the parade." She sucked in a noisy breath. "And for the fireworks," she said, her face scrunched as though in pain. "I miss them." Her lower lip trembled as Trisha engulfed her in a tight hug.

The marching band passed, playing a tune. Individual pieces of wrapped candy dropped around them. "I'm so sorry," Trisha whispered in the girl's ear. Her heart simply shattered when any of the kids acknowledged Parker or Avery with tears in their eyes. Just last night, they'd talked about their parents at the dinner table. Walker had shared the story about how they'd met. Trisha had shared wedding day details. The kids had listened in rapt silence, smiles all around. The children deserved to have the memory of their sweet and loving parents kept alive by Trisha and Walker.

Sophie pulled away. "Thanks, Tish." She swiped a tear off her cheek. "I'm gonna get candy now."

As Trisha stood, Sophie gathered sweets and crammed them in her pockets.

The decorated floats and marching groups kept parading by. Walker's hand brushed over hers again. On purpose?

The past month with him had been wonderful. They worked well together, not only with the horses but also with the children.

Autumn whispered, "What's going on between you and my brother?"

Her eyes widened. "Nothing." Except Trisha couldn't help but recall that almost-kiss from last week while they'd been at the pool and planning the horse show. Had he almost kissed her, or was she making too much of when he'd stared at her?

Autumn didn't look like she believed her but, thankfully, didn't press the issue.

What if their romance bloomed? Trisha had never had a successful relationship because men had either cheated on her or dumped her. Their behavior had convinced her something was wrong with her. But what if there wasn't? What if the problem had been those men?

Walker's actions and words this past month had endeared him to her, and that scared her.

Gabby jostled her. "I'm tired." Trisha leaned down and picked up the girl. She hadn't slept well last night, and at breakfast, she'd told Trisha she'd dreamed of this past Christmas. With her parents. Trisha's heart broke for her. Gabby twined her arms around Trisha's neck and snuggled her head against the fabric of her shirt.

Maybe pursuing her interest in Walker was a bad idea.

The children needed two solid guardians, not a couple who had attempted a romance, failed and ended up with an awkward relationship.

Music thumped as a group of dancers paraded past, signaling the end of the parade. They tossed the last bits of candy to the onlookers. "Want a piece?" she asked Gabby.

"No." The little girl buried her face deeper in Trisha's shirt.

Between the humid day and holding a four-year-old, sweat clung to the insides of Trisha's elbows and beaded on her lower back. The crowd dispersed, and Sophie and Tommy flocked over to them.

"What do you think of Serenity Stables?" Autumn asked Sophie. The two joined hands like they were life-long friends. Trisha was thankful Walker's sister had stayed with them after the parade, because she could tell Sophie's countenance was still a little sad.

At the question, Sophie brightened and chatted about her favorite horses and dogs, and her favorite chore, feeding hay slices at lunchtime. This was the happiest she had appeared all day. "I want to go to college for Ag Science, like Tish, and then come back and help run the horse farm."

Be still, my heart.

Trisha widened her eyes and glanced at Walker. The look they shared spoke volumes. Sophie was happy. Who knew why—maybe it was the farm, perhaps they were doing something right—but Trisha couldn't ask for more.

Later tonight she'd reply to DP Spivey and inform him she had a conflict and would be unable to present in his place. There would likely be other professional opportunities, but right now these children, the horse farm, needed her.

"Want me to hold her?" Walker swept a hand over Gabby's bangs. His hand stilled and his face grew concerned. "I think she has a fever." He reached out to take her; Trisha's skin tingled where his fingers touched her.

Trisha felt Gabby's clammy forehead. How had she not noticed that earlier? "You're right. We should go home."

"No!" Sophie and Tommy cried. "We want to stay."

Trisha met Walker's gaze. They had talked about being a united front and about not giving in. That the adults made the rules, not the children. But today was a special day, so she quirked a smile at him and he nodded.

"Okay," he said as he shifted a now-sleeping Gabby in his arms. "I'll grab my dad and have him run us home. You guys can stay with Trisha and watch the fireworks with the family from the football field."

As the McCaw gang finished collecting chairs and debris from their parade spot, Sophie and Tommy discussed what they wanted to eat from the food trucks.

The only problem with Walker doing the right thing was that now he wouldn't be with them for the light show later on. She'd really been looking forward to watching the fireworks beside Walker.

After checking that Gabby was still sleeping and thankfully felt much cooler, Walker stepped into the dim family room. The television, running the preshow before the fireworks display, was the only light flickering in the room.

Lonely, he crossed the room to settle in for the big event. So, his big brother was going to be a father again. A smile lifted the corners of his lips. The pride in Ethan's eyes as he'd touched Laney's stomach and announced their pregnancy had been heartwarming. Every man should be so blessed, yet that scene had left Walker wanting a life like his brother's. A wife and children with that special someone.

He shook the crazy thought from his head and sat on the couch, pulling the lever to raise his feet. He was so blessed with three sweet children to care for, he shouldn't be looking for more.

Yet he missed Trisha. How had she become such a large part of his life in such a short amount of time? He hadn't had the nerve to take her hand in broad daylight with the kids and his family nearby. But, oh, how he had wanted to.

Music rose from the television. Shots of the crowds waiting for the light show attempted to lure him into the program. Instead, the emptiness of the family room played on his nerves.

He wanted to be with Trisha. Craved spending the special evening with her and the kids. At the memory of their last Friday movie night, he grinned. By creating that tradition, it had forced Walker to slow down and come in from the barn before nightfall. It didn't hurt that the kids always congregated on the carpet, leaving Walker and Trisha no choice but to share the couch.

Trisha made him wildly happy. There, he'd said it. He wasn't sure exactly what made them work so well. On the one hand, he was analytical and she was more adventurous. They shared a faith, worked well as a team, and both loved and were committed to the children. Except his stomach quaked in fear of loving again and possibly losing.

Gravel crunched in the drive. He straightened, then peeked out the window into the dusky night. His heart quickened at the sight of his truck, with Trisha and the kids getting out.

Trisha burst into the house, Tommy and Sophie at her heels, his mother following behind. "We're here to break you out. Your mom is going to stay with Gabby and we can go back to the football field with your family."

Trisha had thought of him. Kind of like he'd been ruminating about her.

"No," he answered. "We'll never find a parking spot in town this late, but I know a place where we can park and watch."

After he thanked his mother and informed her Gabby's fever was much lower, they headed out the front door.

Walker opened the passenger door for Trisha, slid in behind the wheel and checked to make sure the kids' seat belts were buckled. Why had he opened her door? He mentally smacked his palm against his forehead. Would she read anything into it? He focused on the road in front of him, traversed to a lane just outside of town and parked. This was not a date, just two friends hanging out.

"I'd rather be on the football field with the rest of the town, but this is better than nothing," Trisha stated after he parked. She grabbed the quilt they had packed earlier in the day.

He stepped out of the truck, thinking he preferred this isolated road to a field of curious family members and neighbors. He rounded the vehicle and pulled down the tailgate. The kids scampered to the back of the truck.

"Where do you think the fireworks will be?" Trisha gazed off into the distance.

He pointed at the sky. "We should be able to see them clear as day from the bed of the truck." He helped her spread the quilt up against the cab. The kids scrambled to sit on each end, leaving the middle for him and Trisha. The way Sophie deliberately sat on the opposite side from her brother made Walker wonder if the seven-year-old was trying to play matchmaker. He smiled at the notion.

All four of them squished together against the cab of the truck, and he sighed in contentment. It couldn't have been any better.

Sophie tilted her little head against his shoulder and he slipped his arm around her and squeezed. "Walka, I love you," she whispered. The soft words nearly brought Walker to his knees.

"Fireflies," Tommy said. He jumped out of the back of the truck and started chasing them. Sophie followed. Walker settled in the evening silence, allowing Sophie's sweet sentiment to wind around his heart.

With the kids preoccupied, and the light show a good fifteen minutes away, he reached for Trisha's hand. Warmth threaded through him at her touch. She intrigued him. Challenged him. Maybe most important, she listened to him and really heard what he had to say.

She leaned closer and he breathed in her clean scent. "Sophie was upset earlier because this was the first Fourth of July without their parents."

"Ugh. How is she now?"

"Good, I think. Teary for a moment and all, but bounced back much quicker than she would have a few months ago."

Tommy shrieked and then Sophie cackled. Trisha and Walker shared a smile.

"Glad to hear that. I've been praying for them to remember their parents, but also to move on and live their lives. Without guilt." He knew all about guilt.

"It's hard growing up without a mother. You know my mother died when I was Sophie's age." The catch in her voice tugged at him. "Since she had been sick for years, I wasn't really parented, but at least she was there."

He squeezed her hand. "I'm so sorry. That had to be rough."

She sighed. "When my dad jumped from woman to woman, I don't think I ever learned the right way to have a relationship with a man. And you know how burned I felt when Foster dumped me."

Walker's blood boiled at the mention of Foster's name. He'd gone to college with the man and had agreed to be a groomsman for the guy. Then, with no warning, Foster had called off the wedding. "I'm sorry. I still feel bad about that." The announcement had taken everyone by surprise. Apparently, Foster had two sides to him. Their college friend group was only familiar with the kind side of Foster until he broke Trisha's heart.

She bumped him with her shoulder. "It wasn't your fault. Our friends were amazing during that time."

Her words about not being to blame soothed him, though he still felt bad Foster had hurt her. Walker had never understood what the two of them had in common. Foster's degree was in finance and he'd talked about moving to North Carolina for a job after graduation. How had Foster expected that to work if Trisha was employed by his parents in Texas?

The cicada buzz ebbed and flowed as the males worked to woo the females.

Trisha tipped her head against his shoulder.

"I never understood what you saw in him."

"I'm just thankful Foster broke it off when he did rather than go through with it." Her voice warbled. "Because it's clear we never would have worked."

"He had no idea what he was walking away from."

Trisha reached up and touched his face. "Do you really believe that?" His pulse kicked higher as he leaned his forehead against hers. How had he come to care so deeply for her in such a short amount of time?

At the pounding of feet, they shot apart.

Tommy rushed over. "See my firefly?" He opened his cupped palms and a lightning bug flew away.

"Good job, buddy," Walker said. Tommy ran back to his sister to catch more.

Trisha cleared her throat as a long moment passed. The moonlight touched her face with a faint glow.

"You know the hardest part about the breakup?" she said. "Not being able to have my dream job at his parents' horse farm."

He jerked his head back. "I thought you went to Iowa because you wanted to teach."

"No. I wanted to get away from Foster and his family. They crushed my heart when they withdrew my job offer at Harmony Equestrian Center." Her chin quivered with the hard memory.

Had she moved away from Texas because Foster's parents had stolen her confidence in managing a barn?

"Now you're a successful barn manager."

She turned to him and grinned, her eyes sparkling. "You're right, and Serenity Stables suits me way better than the hoity-toity Harmony Equestrian Center." She blew a breath, and a lock of hair shifted away from her face. "This summer God's been teaching me a lot, and one thing is that He's got my back. Even with the broken engagement, He never left me."

A light breeze brought the smell of hay to the air.

"Sounds like God has been working on both of us this summer."

In the darkness, he could see her twirling her hair. A habit she had when nervous.

He couldn't tear his gaze from her kissable lips. So soft and inviting.

"You know, all those terrible experiences have scared me and I'm kind of afraid of…" She lifted their entwined hands. "This." She squeezed tighter, perhaps her way of letting him know she didn't want their hands to part. "My past has taught me I'm not worthy. But God's pushing me to put that doubt behind me."

"I get that." Walker had tried to walk in his own power since the car accident and it had gotten him nothing. His spine lengthened. Recently, he had chosen a different strength. The strength of surrendering. "He has me walking by faith and no longer by sight."

"I've seen a marked difference this past week." Respect shone in her eyes.

Ever since that prayer, he'd felt different. He would submit to Jesus and trust Him, no matter what.

He eyed their clasped hands and considered her trepidation about the two of them.

"Well, you know my struggles since losing Phoebe, so I'm kind of afraid too. Maybe we can be afraid together?" He couldn't tell her his biggest fear—that he would love again and something would happen and he'd be unable to protect her. Just like the car accident.

She leaned her head against his shoulder and a strand of her hair tickled his nose. Her nearness made his senses spin.

Ever since the accident, his life had been like a well-oiled machine. Even after the helicopter crash, when he'd taken custody of the kids, he'd had a semblance of control.

But these past few weeks, his life had been chaotic. Unpredictable and fun.

For the first time in a very long time, he felt like he belonged to a tribe.

"Things seem to be coming together for the show," Trisha said.

"There's a lot of buzz about the flyer you printed for the meet and greet." She smiled up at him, but the tension about saving the farm filled the humid air around them, smothering all other conversations.

Because if that meet and greet wasn't the success Trisha hoped, then they would have failed the children, and Parker and Avery.

The first firework went off with a boom, emitting a dazzling red spray in the distance. The kids raced into the truck and settled beside them, oohing and aahing at the vivid display.

He pushed the importance of the horse show out of his mind. There was nothing he could do about it right now but pray.

As the boom of more colorful fireworks exploded in the sky, he rubbed his thumb across the back of Trisha's hand, enjoying their time together. The mild breeze carried the flinty smell of fireworks.

Should he give romance another shot? Or had he had his one chance with Phoebe?

His head told him to pass on any romantic relationships, but his heart skipped forward, showing him a future with Trisha and the children living like an actual family at Serenity Stables.

Chapter Ten

The Friday after the fireworks, Walker reviewed Chase's résumé once more. Man, the guy looked ideal for the role of barn manager. If only he was as impressive in person and expressed interest in working at Serenity Stables. Walker leaned back and the old office chair squeaked. When they'd first moved here, the noise had irritated him, but now it comforted him.

He felt silly interviewing Chase for the role when they might lose the farm, but in case the meet and greet went as well as Trisha hoped, he wanted to be prepared for her return to Iowa. The timing was right because Chase was looking to move in mid-August.

A stiff breeze blew through the open window as though a storm might be brewing. Boarders strolled past with tack and chatted with one another. He wiggled his fingers at a set of twins passing by. He was amazed at how much business Trisha had drummed up by word of mouth.

Trisha rushed by, carrying a gleaming saddle, probably getting the new horse ready to show to the potential rider interested in leasing. Hopefully, they'd sign, because purchasing two lease horses on spec had not been his plan. But when Trisha had turned those mesmerizing eyes on his, and talked him into how it made business sense, he'd had a hard time refusing.

The other night, when she'd leaned her head against his shoulder, everything seemed perfect. Her soft hand in his connected them in a way he never thought he'd feel again. He was starting to care deeply for her, and no matter how much he didn't want to like her, he did like her. A lot.

Sophie sauntered in, wearing her new brown Western boots with embroidered floral stitching on the foot and shaft. Before Trisha had arrived at the farm, the kids were running around the property in their sneakers. Thankfully, she'd thought to take them to Wild Willie's Western Store and let them each pick out cowboy boots and hats.

"I have an interview in a couple of minutes, sweetie. What can I do for you?"

She held up a finger. "First, stop and smell the roses." Her stern expression cracked him up.

"I don't think your name is Trisha." He held back a grin as he leaned low so they'd be at eye level.

"Now, listen and don't interrupt, okay?" Where'd Sophie pick up on these terms?

"Riley Girl is going to have babies, a whole mess of them, and Chief says we can each have one. Can we please?" She drew out the vowels in desperation.

"No, sweetie, we've got too much happening right now. Maybe next year." He'd told Wilbur no. How come the older man was enticing the children?

She tilted her head. "That's what Tish said." Her lower lip plumped out with a pout.

Thankfully, their unified front continued. He'd half thought Trisha would break ranks and cave in to the kids on this topic.

"Speaking of Tish," Sophie said as she maneuvered into his lap, almost like she was sitting with Santa, asking for Christmas gifts. A seriousness sat in her eyes that he'd not seen in this seven-year-old yet. "I saw you and Tish at the pool, and it looked like you were going to kiss her. Do you like her?"

He felt the heat rise in his neck. "Of course. Your mommy and daddy wanted both of us to be in your lives. Trisha is a good friend."

"So, you hold a friend's hand during the fireworks show?" She lifted her brows with the suggestion only a teenager would understand.

He shifted at the uncomfortable turn this discussion had taken. "We're good friends," he reiterated. Tonight was family movie night, and he didn't want to admit how much he was looking forward to sitting beside Trisha and sharing popcorn while the kids ended up falling fast asleep because playing outside all day had exhausted them.

After Sophie hopped down, she smoothed her shorts. "Well, us kids wouldn't mind if you and Tish got married. Just sayin'." With that bit of wisdom, and maybe hope, she darted away.

He steepled his hands and leaned into his index fingers. Since the children were his top priority, he'd been concerned about getting involved with Trisha, but now he had their blessing.

His mind traveled back to the other night. Settled against the cab of his truck, while watching the fireworks with Trisha leaning against his shoulder and their hands intertwined—the evening had been flawless.

The instant she had opened up to him about the fear she held about pursuing another, something in his mind had clicked. So when they'd agreed to be afraid together, it almost felt like they shared a secret bond.

"Hey, you."

Trisha leaned into the office. With her hair mussed, ruddy cheeks from working hard and likely dirt under her nubby nails, she looked great. "They signed the lease." Her look screamed, *I told you so.*

He stood. "Awesome. I believed in you."

She pulled a face and turned.

"Remember I told you about the hay fields we aren't using?"

Her face lit up. "Yes?"

"Henry, from down the street, said he'd be interested. Twice a year." He named the price they'd agreed to, and her brows rose.

"That's great news." She rushed over and threw her arms around him in a celebratory hug. His heart pounded a quickstep in his chest at their closeness.

He closed his eyes to enjoy the moment and caught a hint of her shampoo before she stepped back.

"Sorry about that, boss." Her cheeks flamed.

Right. She meant nothing by it except excitement over their bottom line, and that was okay. Really.

He remembered how reluctant she'd been to become the barn manager. She and the kids had expected to spend quality time together, but somehow Trisha had integrated the children into their daily work lives. It was great for the children to be challenged and have chores, but more importantly, this was the happiest and most content the kids had been since their parents' memorial service. He honestly hadn't believed they'd ever come this far. His phone dinged with a reminder about Chase's arrival.

"Are you still available for the interview in about five minutes?"

"Yup." She strode away. But before she'd turned, an irritable look had overtaken her face.

He cocked his head. They hadn't interacted a ton since the fireworks show. Maybe she hadn't enjoyed holding hands after all, though he'd enjoyed it immensely.

His prayer last week had loosened the load on his shoulders. He'd been living in the past too long. Now he needed to live in the present and maybe put himself out there. He liked Trisha, but did she like him?

If the only relationship they had was raising the children and working together at the farm, he'd be okay with that. Because the few weeks he'd been here before she had arrived had been pure torture. He'd been out of his element, almost frozen with fear about how to make the farm profitable.

But then Trisha had arrived and somehow turned a scary situation into an enjoyable adventure. Not only for him, but for the kids.

"Knock, knock."

Startled, he looked up. A young man, who nervously shifted his worn Stetson on his head, stood there.

Walker strode to the door and extended his hand. "You must be Chase."

They shook hands and got settled. "So tell me a little about yourself." Everything Chase said fit perfectly into Serenity Stables. Walker rubbed his hands in glee. Finally, everything was coming together. After Trisha went back to Iowa, they'd have a barn manager, and with the news of the leased horse, they weren't stretched as thin. Assuming the horse show had a favorable outcome.

"Sounds like you'd fit in here nicely. What do you do

at your current job?" His gaze flitted to the aisle. Where was Trisha?

Just when Chase got to his daily duties, Trisha slipped in and Walker introduced them.

He noticed Trisha's handshake was limp, and instead of sitting down and engaging, she hovered in the corner and typed on her phone. Her lips were pressed together, which she did when she was upset, though he doubted she realized it. He had no idea what was going on in her head, but right now they had a live candidate who was a good possibility.

What was wrong with her? Her behavior was so unlike her daily countenance. Had he said something to offend her? Was something wrong with one of the kids?

Walker gave a mental shake of his head. Usually, they worked so well together, kind of like a well-oiled machine. Not today. Or, at least, not right now.

He put Trisha's attitude aside and conducted the rest of the interview with minimal interaction from her. Chase's résumé had been promising, and he sounded ideal in person. Maybe they'd found their new barn manager with just one interview.

Walker described the apartment above the garage, and Trisha cleared her throat. What? She would be living in Iowa by the time Chase moved in. They needed to throw every benefit at Chase to secure his employment because the salary wasn't as high as what the man was currently making.

"How many hands are here to help?"

"Two," Walker answered.

"They here every day?"

"If they feel like it," Trisha stated.

What? "No, what Trisha means is that occasionally

they are off. There's a schedule and they alternate week-end days with each other." He glared at her, but she fo-cused on her phone. Was she trying to scare off the man?

If the horse show was a success, then the kids could grow up here like their parents wanted, but they couldn't succeed without a barn manager. A good one.

At the end of the interview, Chase didn't have ques-tions. Was that a bad thing? Walker had hoped he'd be a bit more engaged. So Walker gave the man a tour of the property, including the garage apartment Trisha had re-luctantly said he could show.

"That's a way nicer apartment than I have right now," Chase chuckled. As they stepped off the last tread, their boots crunched on the crushed gravel. Big puffy clouds filled the sky and the air smelled like rain.

Skeeter raced over and jumped at Walker's knees. He leaned down and rubbed the scruff of his neck. Riley Girl waddled over, her stubby tail wagging at warp speed.

Regardless of how cute these dogs were, Walker's de-cision stood firm. They had way too much on their plate without adding a puppy, or three, to the family.

But then Sophie's pout flitted through his mind. He hoped his firm answer had spoken to her, otherwise those tenacious kids might wear him down and persuade him to bring a puppy, or three, home. And that would be complete chaos.

"I'm going to be honest," Chase said as he dug the toe of his boot into the gravel. "I couldn't help but notice Trisha doesn't seem to want me here, and I really don't want to leave my current job for a new one full of drama."

"No, no, it isn't anything like that. She's having a bad day and actually lives in Iowa, so she won't be a part of our everyday operation after Labor Day." For the life of him, Walker didn't know why Trisha was hindering the hire of this perfect barn manager.

Chase worked his jaw back and forth. "Then I'll think about it." They shook hands, and Chase drove away.

Why did Walker think he'd never hear from the man again? His frustration with Trisha had built while he'd toured the property with Chase. Right now, it felt like his head was going to pop off.

What was wrong with her?

Later that afternoon, Trisha clucked to get the horse moving. Until someone fully leased the new horses they had bought, she'd have to work them out every day. She trotted in a circle, then squeezed her heels, and the horse cantered while she moved her body in rhythm with the gait.

Was Chase gone yet? Had Walker offered him the barn manager position already? She hoped not.

She tugged on the reins and made a figure eight to reverse direction and force the horse to change leads. He did a beautiful job.

Try as she might, she could not get the image of her and Walker all cozy and holding hands on the Fourth of July out of her mind. When she was with him, she felt safe and secure. Something about this farm or the kids or the house or their budding relationship made her feel like she was finally home. And it felt good.

Why had she shared her deep secrets with Walker the other night? Of course, he'd known most of it because he'd been part of her friend group in college. But did he now see her as the loser she saw herself?

She moved with the horse's gait. Boy, she missed this. Why had she given up riding when she'd moved to Iowa? Had she changed her life plans because she'd loved teaching or because she'd wanted to create as much space as possible between her and Foster and his successful family stables?

As a group class filed into the ring, she pulled up. She might as well finish this workout indoors because she didn't want to be in Amanda's way.

"Someday I'm going to ride like that," Sophie stated from her perch on the fence railing. A bit of awe clung to her tone.

Trisha stopped in front of the girl. She hadn't noticed her there. "You're not too far off, kiddo. You have a beautiful seat, just like your mama did."

Sophie's lips quivered and tears sprang to her eyes.

Oh no. Trisha hadn't meant to upset the girl.

"Really?" Instead of pain, Trisha saw hope and excitement on her face. "Did you ride with her?" she whispered.

Trisha dismounted, pulled the reins over the horse's ears and started walking to the gate. Sophie trailed along on the other side of the fence. "Sure did. We worked at the Triple C in the summers during college and used our paychecks to enter a couple of shows. She was good." She laughed. "Better than me."

Trisha walked through the gate and joined the girl.

"Walka said no to the puppies," Sophie stated. "He didn't even think about it." She sniffed, a frown covering her face.

"We talked about this last night, sweetie. There have been lots of changes recently and now may not be the best time to bring a little puppy into the family."

"Puppies," Sophie said as she glared at her. "Chief said we could each have one. I already named mine. Spot, or Daisey if I get a girl."

Trisha held back a chuckle at her exuberance. She'd

have to remind Wilbur that Walker wasn't interested in the work that came with puppies.

"You could change his mind." Sophie looked up at her with such hope.

"I think he's already decided, sweetie." Trisha wrapped the reins around her hand. "Why don't you help me untack Viking? I want to see if you can reach the saddle."

"I can reach. I know I can." Sophie puffed her chest out as they made their way to the upper barn.

These children were so sweet and helpful. She thanked God that the worst days of grieving seemed to be behind them.

Once in the center aisle, she slid Viking's bridle off, replaced it with a halter and hooked him to the cross-ties. "Okay, big girl, let me see what you've got."

First, Sophie slid the stirrups up the leather, then lifted the saddle flap and unhooked the girth. Finally, she stood on tiptoe as she precariously pulled the saddle and pad off the horse. "Got it," she called as she fast-walked over to the tack room to put it away.

Spontaneous tears formed in Trisha's eyes. Avery's oldest might very well stay on to manage the farm when she grew up—assuming the show was as successful as she hoped and they got to keep the stable.

"I did it. Tish, I did it." An excited Sophie threw her arms around Trisha.

"Want to brush him?"

"Yes, ma'am." Sophie took the brush, but didn't move. "Why do you live in Iowa?"

Trisha made sure her smile didn't slip. The kid sure asked a great question. One she'd been asking herself more and more lately. "Because that's where my job is." Why was she so afraid of coming back to Texas permanently? If she moved here, she'd be part of the children's everyday lives, have a chance at having close female friends, be an integral part of this family and the Mc-Caws, and maybe she and Walker could give a relationship a try. If she were honest with herself, she loved being the barn manager way more than teaching her students.

The realization hit her with a thud.

Why had she let her ex-fiancé disrupt her life so, and how come it had taken her so long to realize the truth?

She had spent eight years doing something that wasn't her dream. Regret knifed at her. She had some serious praying to do.

If she decided this was where she wanted to be, would Walker let her stay on as barn manager or was he set on Chase? She shook off the notion. She'd handle that later.

Viking shuddered and stepped away.

"Why'd he do that?" Sophie held the brush in the palm of her tiny hand.

Trisha smiled. "Sometimes horses do that when they're ticklish. I've noticed Viking's left rump is sensitive."

Her brows squished together. "So what do I do?"

"Just move over here and start again." Trisha pointed, but Sophie twirled the brush in her hands as though thinking.

"Do you like Walka?"

Trisha stilled, and then a giggle erupted from her throat. "Of course I do, silly. We're friends." She moved to the other side of Viking so Sophie couldn't see the heat flaming her cheeks.

Sophie followed. "It's okay if you do. We'd really like you to stay."

Wait. Walker wanted her to stick around? "Who have you been talking with?"

"Tommy and Gabby. We like it with you here. Since you came, Walka stops to smell the roses." She lifted her chin.

So the girl had been eavesdropping, huh?

A painful lump lodged in her throat that Walker wasn't the one who wanted her to stay.

"There you are," Walker called from the mouth of the barn. "What did you think of Chase?" He frowned as he stepped toward her, likely because of her not-so-friendly behavior toward Chase earlier.

"He was okay." She simply had to talk him out of hiring Chase because Trisha wanted the job. The kids even wanted her here, which she'd never expected. How could she gently nudge Walker away from Chase, the ideal candidate, when Trisha had a thriving career in Iowa?

"There's Bella and Arielle's sister," Sophie stated. She handed Trisha the brush. "Gotta go." She hurried off to join the other girl.

"He's a little young, don't you think?" she said.

Lines appeared between Walker's eyebrows. "He's older than we are. Personally, I thought he was great."

Did that mean he didn't believe she'd do a good job as barn manager long-term? "He seemed concerned about how much help he'd get, almost like he wasn't used to doing the work himself, and around here, he'd have to work hard." She should know. She dropped into bed every night, thoroughly exhausted. Yet it felt so good.

His lips thinned. "Trisha, I don't know what you were doing in there, but you may have bungled the whole thing."

That was her hope. She lifted her chin.

"Because of you, we may never hear from the perfect barn manager candidate."

"You thought he was perfect?"

Walker plucked his Stetson off his head and ran a

frustrated hand through his deliciously messed-up hair. "Of course I did. And, Trisha, you're making no sense." He turned and marched away.

"Wait." She had to tell him. He deserved to know why she'd tried to sabotage the interview, and she wanted to know if he'd keep her on.

He turned, his lips pursed.

She moved closer so no one would hear, just in case he hated the idea. But he'd like it, right? She was good at the barn and the kids liked her. They were thriving this summer, doing much better than any of them thought they'd do with this change.

She gulped. "How about if I stayed on as barn manager?" she whispered.

He stared at her, then started shaking his head. "You'd give up your booming collegiate career for this?" He spread his arms open to Serenity Stables. "I don't think so." He chuckled, turned and walked away.

So, she wasn't worthy enough to hold the position long-term.

Fuming, she put Viking back in his stall with fresh water and a slice of hay. She wanted to stomp away, but she didn't want to scare the horses. Instead, she rushed out to the pasture, and as soon as her boots hit the gravel, she broke into a run and raced away her frustrations over Walker.

She allowed tears to stream over her face and didn't bother to wipe them away.

Why was she never good enough? No matter how hard she tried, she wasn't deemed worthy enough.

Here she'd thought Walker believed in her. Trusted her. Thought she was doing a fabulous job.

Apparently, he'd been pretending until he found someone to replace her with.

Chapter Eleven

As Trisha strode to the outside ring with Amanda, Ryder, Buck and Walker, her hair blew around her face. The kids were at Cora's for a few hours so they could focus on setting up the dry run of the course for the Sunday jumper classes.

The last couple of weeks had flown by in a blur. With the children, the daily horse farm activities and preparing for the horse show, the only downtime had been church and family dinners.

Of course, she and Walker had been tap-dancing with the maybe-relationship between them. Or perhaps it was all in her head? She shook the romance thoughts away and gripped the clipboard in her hand.

"Let's just get the standards in place. Then we can add the rails," she said to Ryder and Buck. They maneuvered the PVC posts that would hold the rails in place. Walker followed close behind. His enticing smell drifted toward her each time he got too close. Amanda and the stable hands were ample help. He didn't really need to be here.

But ever since that interview with Chase, he'd been... remorseful? She wasn't sure. But if he was, he'd be spot-on.

She was shocked at how he had dismissed her when she'd told him she wanted to stay on as barn manager.

He was clueless or just plain mean. Regardless, she didn't have the bandwidth to deal with him right now. She was mad at him and missed him all at the same time.

While she waited for the standards to be moved, she tucked her long hair into a crude ponytail. She wiggled her fingers at a few riders making their way into a pasture that Ryder and Buck had leveled and turned into a temporary riding ring.

How could they only be five days away from the horse show? She shook her head. She'd probably forgotten a ton of tiny details, but she thought she had a handle on all the big things. At least Kent was still on for the meet and greet that she had high hopes would collect enough money to keep Serenity Stables going.

When she stopped, Walker bumped into her. She turned and glared at him, then pointed to where the next set of standards was to be placed. Walker stepped back, a worried look on his face.

"Don't you have anything else to do today?" Like maybe call or text his precious, perfect barn manager? For a moment, she wondered if Chase had ever gotten back to him. If Walker had actually offered him the job, when was he starting? When was he moving into her apartment?

But no, it was none of her business. If the show succeeded, they needed to move forward as though they'd keep the farm, and she'd signed on only to help for the summer. That was it. She had a life in Iowa to return to, which Walker had clearly reminded her of.

Trisha consulted her clipboard, the wind blew the paper up, again, and she slapped it down. She looked at the printed course map and noted the next area for the standards. Ryder and Buck rushed off to get more while Amanda put cups in the slots of the standards. What would she do without these employees? The staff the prior owners had left, other than Roy, were so helpful.

Using her stride to count the distance between the jumps, she moved on to the next cross-rail, while Walker awkwardly used a tape measure.

"How did you do that?" he asked as he released the end of the tape and it clicked back into place. "Thirty-six feet and you measured that perfectly just by walking it."

"Years of practice."

"Did you draw that course up on your own?" Walker motioned to her clipboard that held five sheets of paper representing the variety of jumping classes they were planning to hold.

"No, Walker. This is an accredited show with the points system. There is a protocol to follow. I got this from their website." Her tone came out a little too sharp.

Maybe being irritated with him wasn't the way to snag the barn manager position. Perhaps she should tell him what she wanted? Again.

No, she didn't have the guts. Clearly, he didn't believe she was good enough to stay on.

He touched her elbow and her breath stalled in her lungs. How could she have feelings for him and be mad at him at the same time?

She turned. His cowboy hat shaded his features but she could still see the worry lines on his face. Part of her wanted to smooth the wrinkles away with her fingertips. The other part of her just wanted him to leave her alone so she could forget he didn't deem her worthy enough for the role.

"What's wrong?" he asked. "For the past few weeks, you've been acting angry toward me."

It had all started on the day of Chase's interview when she'd told him she'd wanted to stay. His laughter and disbelief that she'd pick this over academia had hurt all over again. The memory had been on an endless loop ever since it had happened.

No, she wouldn't bring it up for fear that she'd read his laughter correctly and he didn't think she'd make a good enough permanent barn manager.

"No, Walker, this is me in panic mode." A frustrated sigh erupted from her throat. "You usually do this dry run like a month or two before the show date, not five days." She hoped he bought her faked excuse. It was pretty plausible.

These past few weeks, she'd been nervous every morning that Chase would arrive to take over her role. With each passing day, her hope of staying strengthened. But Walker had just likely earmarked Chase to start right before she headed back home, which made sense. Why pay Chase when she'd work for free? Dread coursed through her like a slithering snake.

"How come you've been heading off to bed as soon as the kids go down lately?"

"I've been tired." She spread her arms wide, almost losing her grip on the clipboard. "And we've been working extra hard on this, remember?" She turned her gaze to the stable hands so Walker wouldn't see the sudden sheen in her eyes.

She'd missed spending time with him on the porch to talk about their days and just connect, but she couldn't allow herself to fall for him any more than she already had. Not being with him was torture. Being around him was almost worse.

He didn't understand that she'd give up her life in academia for this. In fact, she couldn't even remember what the draw had been to teach at a college in Iowa, other than to get away from her ex-fiancé.

She cringed just considering that time in her life and her quick life decisions.

Walker moved in front of her. "Trisha." He lifted her chin with his index finger. The feel of his skin against hers was like water during a drought. Her chest gave a tight squeeze. Oh, how she missed him. It took everything in her power not to press her eyes closed and lean into him.

"I'm not talking about this dry run," he said. Those worry lines seemed to etch deeper into his tanned skin. "Seems ever since the day we interviewed Chase, you've been angry with me. Why?"

For a moment, she fidgeted, but then she realized this was her chance. She gulped, balanced the clipboard on top of a standard and said a quick prayer that he wouldn't laugh at her again. "I think I really want the barn manager position." After she'd whispered her hopes and dreams, she studied the dirt below her boots. "The day Chase was here, you laughed at me."

His face turned somber. "Oh my. Trisha, I wasn't laughing at you. Not at all." He took her hands in his. "I am so sorry. I guess your comment surprised me because your career is skyrocketing, what with that promotion you got in May."

She cocked her head because she hadn't mentioned the promotion to anyone.

He rubbed his rough-skinned thumb against the back

of her hand. "I'm so sorry for my outburst that day. I didn't mean it, and I apologize."

Hadn't meant it? Her thoughts jumbled together. "Really? I figured you thought I wasn't good enough." Just like Foster and Foster's parents. If she were being honest, her parents had treated her that way as well. She tried not to squirm, but if she'd learned nothing else this summer, it was that God had her back. If Walker thought she couldn't handle the position and she had to return to Iowa, she'd be okay.

He tilted his head, remorse covering his features. "Oh, Trisha, you are more than good enough. You've miraculously transformed these stables into a beehive of activity, and you came up with the meet-and-greet idea that's going to save Serenity Stables. I can't think of anyone who would be better than you at managing this place."

Her heart soared with his confidence and the possibility of staying, being able to truly settle in and call this place home. She had already put herself out there with him romantically. In fact, she was falling for him as her emotions spiraled out of control. He would either reject her or something amazing would happen. She hoped for the amazing option.

"I'd love you to stay, and I know for a fact the kids would as well. But are you sure? You have an incredible career in Iowa."

"Where to, boss?" Buck interrupted.

Trisha grabbed her clipboard, reviewed the drawing and pointed to the spot for the next set of jumps. "I love the university," she told Walker. "But I think this summer has taught me this is my dream."

She'd never seen a wider grin on his face. Maybe that meant he liked her? Perhaps as much as she was attracted to him?

"Then it's settled. I'll hold off on looking for a barn manager. The job is all yours if you want it, assuming we can make the place profitable."

She bumped her shoulder against his. "Thanks." Tears of joy pricked the backs of her eyelids, but she couldn't linger because, in five days, they had a show to put on. She focused on the task at hand.

The horse show had been so fun to plan and execute. A little crazy, but satisfying. She couldn't wait for Friday, when all the vendors would come and the PA system and bleachers would be set up. Then, early Saturday, the riders and horses would arrive, all excited for their events.

Amanda came alongside her. "Sorry to interrupt, but there's a threat of heavy rain all weekend."

She sucked in a breath as panic slid down her spine. "No."

Amanda nodded. "Ninety percent Saturday. Seventy-five on Sunday."

Oh no, the dirt would turn into a mud pile and riders would fall more easily. What about the equestrians who hadn't yet entered? They might not show and she'd been told that was usually one-third of the participants. Serenity Stables wouldn't collect the entrance fees from them. And what about the vendors? All the extra money she'd thought they'd make, and if it rained like Amanda predicted, they'd barely cover their costs.

What if they had to cancel because of weather? The way the Hunter Jumper Circuit set the show schedule, any rain-delayed events would be rescheduled to the end of the season. Right now, because of the earlier North Texas rainy spring season, that meant November.

The meet and greet with Kent Kelton would fail.

Serenity Stables needed to succeed this weekend. They couldn't wait four more months.

Her stomach coiled into a tight knot. The one thing she couldn't control. Weather.

Walker was kicking himself for the wry chuckle a few weeks ago that had wounded Trisha. He hadn't meant to dismiss her, not at all. He'd truly thought she was joking.

His mouth went dry at the suffering she'd gone through at his hands. She had probably chosen not to chat with him after putting the kids to bed because of her confusion over his hurtful behavior. That must have been the reason she'd been so distant.

Amanda landed the final jump, and he shifted his Stetson. It all made sense now. Hopefully, the Saturday-morning doughnut outings and Friday family movie nights would no longer be uncomfortable with Trisha.

"Let's set this up in the indoor arena. Just in case," Trisha said under her breath. Her jaw tightened as she told the stable hands about the extra work. To their credit, Buck and Ryder didn't flinch, just told her to lead the way.

"They're the best," she said as she told Amanda the new plans and hurried to the indoor arena to replicate the course.

Feeling grateful, Walker followed. Having Trisha as the barn manager would be great, but when the kids learned the news, they'd be ecstatic. Though, he'd let her tell them, as he wasn't sure she was completely on board.

He shook his head. Who left a successful teaching career to work on a horse farm? He never would have guessed she'd truly stay on.

They stepped to the edge of the compacted dirt of the

indoor arena as the stable hands started moving the standards. "You think this'll work?" Walker asked Trisha. Hopefully, she hadn't seen a problem as soon as they'd stepped over the threshold.

Her lips pressed into a tight line. No doubt she was assessing the situation. "We won't be able to use the bleachers if we move the show in here."

It made him feel good she'd liked his bleacher idea. "When do we need to decide?"

"Saturday morning." Her voice was firm. "We'll take each day as they come." Disappointment dulled her eyes.

He caught her hand. "So we're good, right?"

For a moment, confusion filtered over her face before she gave him a shy smile and nodded.

His shoulders relaxed with the good news. It had been a long two weeks not only walking on eggshells around her, but fearing there was no hope for their relationship. He gave her hand a squeeze. "Maybe we should help?" He motioned to Ryder and Buck.

She looked up from her clipboard. "It won't take them long to move everything over here. It's PVC now instead of wood, you know. Back in the old days when I was showing, they made the standards and rails of heavy wood."

These past two weeks had taught him to watch his tongue—in this case, errant laughter. But, more importantly, he had realized how much he cared for Trisha and how much he hoped she'd stay. Not just because she made a great barn manager, but he really liked her and wanted to see if whatever this was between them could be more.

Out of the corner of his eye, he saw Amanda riding Goliath. "It's amazing how you've turned Goliath around.

I never thought that would be a possibility." He pointed at Amanda and the well-controlled horse.

"Give us another month and he'll be up for lease. I've already gotten interest." Her eyes sparkled at the news as she leaned her clipboard against the wall.

"Wow, I applaud you. I never thought Goliath would be anything other than a menace," he said. Then he thought about the auction they'd gone to a month ago. "I certainly didn't want to purchase those two lease horses on spec. But you've made me eat my words on both counts." He nudged her shoulder, though he really wanted to give her a celebratory hug. "Good job, Trisha. You were right."

"Thanks. It's been a lot of fun." She caught her lower lip between her teeth. "You know, it's odd how I thought academia was my dream, but these past couple of weeks I realized when I moved to Iowa I was trying to put as much distance between myself and Foster and that mega-fancy horse farm of theirs." She twisted her college ring, which he'd noticed she only did when talking about her past.

"That's understandable."

"It's cool you figured out your dream was computer security," she said, then turned to direct Ryder and Buck while Walker took a moment to collect himself. She was way off. His dream was absolutely not cybersecurity.

His heart thundered in his chest at the musings he'd been having lately. "I've been working through some things myself too. Took coming here and running this place for me to remember the reason I went to college, and it wasn't my love for computers."

"What do you mean?" She turned her full attention to him.

"I wouldn't say cybersecurity was my dream. More

like I went to college because my dad didn't need five kids helping him at our cattle ranch." He shrugged. "I was one of the youngest, so I figured he didn't need me."

Her face fell. "Wade would never feel that way. Anyway, there's always more to do on a cattle ranch. Or a horse farm. Could you imagine if all three kids wanted to be part of this family business?"

Parker and Avery would be pleased if any or all of the children stayed here after high school or college. Walker knew he would be. Sophie, Tommy and Gabby all loved horses and had shown a keen interest in the workings of the farm this summer.

Walker leaned against the wall. She was right. There'd *always* been something else that needed to be done at the Triple C. His three brothers all worked there now and his dad was always commenting about the never-ending list of things to do.

Something shifted inside and it made him wonder if he'd gone to college twelve years ago out of fear rather than out of interest in cybersecurity. Back then, he had wanted to be something, and being third in command behind his father and older brother at the Triple C wasn't his dream of success.

Trisha's earlier words about giving up her career in academia for barn management filtered through his mind. He straightened. She was right. He'd likely entered the computer industry for the wrong reasons. No wonder it had been on his mind recently, making him feel wholly unsettled.

A breeze shot through the huge open doors and horses neighed in the distance. He knew the hardships of operations director held a different type of stress than his computer job.

Leaving his career would take guts and trusting God. As a sudden dad to three little ones, working on the horse farm made the most sense for them. But was it the right move for him?

"Amanda's almost ready," Trisha stated as Amanda mounted their best hack and Buck led Goliath away. "Let's move to the viewing room to watch."

Deep in thought, he followed her. Ryder and Buck had set up the course exactly as in the outdoor ring.

Trisha touched his fingers. "Whatcha thinking about?" She looked up at him with concern on her face.

"Mulling over what you said about your career." He placed his Stetson back on his head. "I guess things have been so busy since we closed on this place that I haven't slowed down long enough to realize I like being outdoors all day. I've missed manual labor."

Her eyebrow arched. "What are you saying?"

"Maybe this is my dream, not cybersecurity."

The kids clamored in, his mother close behind.

"Riley Girl is whelping!" Sophie announced. "Wilbur said he'd prop his front door open once everyone was all cleaned up and we could see the puppies." Her little face was red with excitement.

Trisha gave him a small smile, as if to say, *They need one.* She had a valid point. But he'd be too overwhelmed, right? Maybe Riley Girl would have another litter next year. Next year, he might feel more composed.

"I can't wait to hold them," Gabby said, a dreamy look on her face.

"It'd be even better if *we* could have them." Sophie rose on her toes. She was adorable when excited. How could Walker keep saying no to them?

"Who knows? Maybe Wilbur won't sell them. Maybe they'll all become barn dogs," Sophie said in a wistful tone.

Trisha caught his eye and raised her brows. She was right. If they were both planning to stay on full-time at the farm, he couldn't say no to the kids.

"Okay, you can have a puppy," Walker relented. The peace and odd excitement that bubbled up felt superb. The children deserved the opportunity to raise a puppy, and what was one little dog, anyway?

"Can we each have one?" Sophie gave him little puppy-dog eyes.

He heard a chuckle from his mother. This right here was a life lesson. He had to accept he wouldn't get his own way, not if he was fathering three children and courting a headstrong, gorgeous woman. He would have to be open to change if it would make the people he cared about happy.

"Okay. Three." The kids erupted in cheers as his mother wiggled her fingers at him and walked out. Trisha gave him an encouraging nod while the kids huddled around to hug and thank him.

"Here we go," Trisha stated, and they all quieted as Amanda rode the variety of courses being offered on Sunday.

Staying on as operations director at the horse farm took up residence in his heart. Each time Amanda landed a jump, he felt more certain about switching his career focus and not returning to his cybersecurity job. Assuming the horse show was the success they'd planned on.

Sophie tugged his hand. He leaned down and she whispered they were going to wait in the far pasture to watch for the open-door signal from Wilbur. She gave him one last excited hug before they tore off.

"Perfect," Trisha murmured as Amanda landed the last jump. She leaned her head against his chest and he put his arm across her shoulder while she snuggled in. This was nice.

Amanda circled before exiting the ring, and Walker realized if he left his computer job, he would not regain his corporate paycheck every month. With the financial struggle these past six months, he'd missed his automated monthly deposit and questioned whether they could survive without an outside income.

For the success of the farm, maybe he should stick with his computer career. After all, their goal was to make sure the kids could keep Serenity Stables and grow up here. Hanging on to his job might be the long-term difference between success and failure. At least for the children.

An errant hair tickled his nose. He tilted his head against Trisha's.

Now that he'd allowed himself to fantasize for a moment, he was unsure he could bottle up his feelings and slam the lid closed on his new dream.

After being rooted in guilt for the past six years, he finally had hope for a future. A bright future.

He slid a glance at Trisha. If they both worked at the farm and their relationship progressed, maybe he could actually have it all.

Chapter Twelve

The cloudy evening didn't hinder the children from being excited about Cora's petting zoo. Goats bleated and pushed their noses against Trisha's hand in search of food, while the miniature horses grunted and snorted to get their attention. A smile tugged Trisha's lips at how satisfied she and the kids were with their life on the horse farm.

Trisha sneaked a glance at Walker. It had been two days since he'd apologized for laughing when she'd mentioned moving here. He wanted her to stay on as barn manager, but she wasn't sure how he felt about her romantically. Her pulse had flickered at the sweet tenderness on his face during their discussion.

He'd told her, *The job is all yours if you want it.* Though that had been a relief, she wondered about them. He hadn't held her hand since Monday. Each time he touched her, she felt wrapped in invisible warmth, and she wanted more of that, but she shouldn't.

Sophie calmly strolled through the spacious pen, petting each animal on her way, not scared in the least.

"Will Pinky Pie bite?" Gabby clung to Trisha's leg, using her as a shield of protection against the cute goat.

"No, sweetie, see?" Trisha let the goat nibble her palm. "Memaw makes sure all the animals are friendly." She adored how Cora and Wade had insisted the kids call them Memaw and Pops, just like their other grandchildren.

Across the pen, Tommy held Walker's big hand. The kids hadn't fully gotten used to country life. Yet. They were comfortable with horses, but these smaller quick animals still made the younger two nervous.

Gabby reached around and touched Pinky Pie's nose, then giggled. "It tickles," she said.

Walker sent her a smirk because he was dealing with the same type of thing with Tommy. They needed to be patient because the children would soon adjust and be as comfortable as their older sister one day.

"It does tickle. Want some grain so you can feed her?"

Gabby's eyes opened wide and then she nodded. Trisha gave her a couple of nuggets and the girl jumped back and tossed them on the ground. "I scawed," she stated.

Trisha popped the girl on her hip and juggled the feedbag in her other hand. Thankfully, Walker noticed her predicament and took the bag from her. His fingers brushed hers and her heart pitter-pattered.

Stop it. The contact means nothing. Except, even though she tried to discount her rising attraction, the touch meant something to her. Was Walker even interested in her?

As they approached the miniature horses, Gabby snuggled her little head against Trisha's collarbone and squeezed her legs tighter. Trisha rubbed her palm against one of their muzzles.

"See how the animals are roaming free?" At her nod, Trisha continued. "They usually huddle under the shade of the pavilion to stay cooler."

"We should get them cowboy hats," Gabby said.

Trisha chuckled. "You're right, sweetie. We should."

Walker crouched beside Tommy, who held his hand out to a goat. The animal munched the offered food, and Tommy reached into the bag for more pellets. Walker was so patient and kind with the kids.

For Wednesday night family dinner, he'd shaved and sported newish blue jeans along with a short-sleeved, blue-checked Western shirt. His hands were tanned to a golden color, but his arms had seen little sunlight.

As Sophie continued to pet each animal, she started singing a praise song from church. With such a pretty voice, she had joined the children's choir earlier in the month and loved it.

Yes, getting all five of them ready earlier than usual tonight had been a challenge, but the kids had been begging to see the small animals. Trisha's heart sighed with contentment.

"I hungwy," Gabby said as she wiggled to get down, then ran over to Walker for him to hold her.

Without a cowboy hat on, Walker looked downright dashing. With his hair parted off to the side, his gentle waves fell around his head. A cowboy holding a cute child. What wasn't to like?

Sophie interrupted her pretty song and raced over to Trisha, throwing her little arms around her waist. "I love living in the country," she announced.

"I do too." Trisha wrapped the girl in a hug, thrilled they'd planned their day so the kids could have this special time with the goats and miniature horses.

Autumn pulled into the parking lot, gave a little wave and then rushed to the big house.

"We should head in now," Walker said.

Later, seated next to Walker around the biggest dining

table she'd ever seen, Trisha pushed her plate away. Her stomach and heart were full. She just loved this family. When she'd agreed to be the backup guardian for Parker and Avery's children, never had she considered that one day she'd become part of the McCaw clan. But because she was coguardian with Walker, the McCaws had once again opened their doors and hearts to her. She'd be eternally grateful for their acceptance and kindness.

"I want to hear about your puppies. Which ones did you pick?" Cora's eyes twinkled with the question she directed at Sophie, Tommy and Gabby.

They talked at once, so Cora told them one at a time, starting with the youngest.

"Mine is the pwettiest in the litter. She's all white except for brown ears and a brown tail." Gabby chewed her bottom lip to keep herself from talking more.

"I named mine Spot," Tommy said. "He's all white except for a brown and a black spot on his back. He's the handsomest of the group." His chest puffed out so far, it touched the wood table.

"I don't mean to disagree with Gabby," Sophie said as she lifted her chin. "But mine is gorgeous. Half her face is white and the other is chocolate brown. She's simply breathtaking."

Trisha pressed her lips together to keep from laughing at the lyrical description of Sophie's puppy.

"Well, I'm excited for each of you and I can't wait to meet them," Cora said, a wide smile on her face.

Trisha felt so honored. She and the kids weren't part of the McCaw family, but Cora and Wade had not only invited them in, they'd made them feel welcome and loved. Though this would continue for the children, if she returned to Iowa, she'd miss this loving family, and she never wanted this satisfying feeling to end.

When Cora pushed back from the table, a chorus of chairs scraped against the hardwood as the rest of the clan stood. Trisha reached for her plate, but Walker got to it first. He gave her a caring glance and she felt a hum of attraction.

"Weather this weekend looks iffy," Autumn said as she made her way into the cramped kitchen. "I'll be praying." A murmur of agreement resounded from the group.

Trisha refused to look at her weather app. Meteorologists weren't always right, and frankly, the date of the show couldn't be changed.

The whole family herded into the kitchen with their plates, silverware and glasses. Everyone helped. Trisha appreciated the men didn't consider it women's work, and she was thankful for the great example the children were being shown.

Still weighing her career in academia against the barn manager role at Serenity Stables, she moved into the kitchen. She'd kind of decided to stay here, but was worried her motivation might be to see if a relationship with Walker panned out. She'd been praying about it, leaving the decision in God's capable hands.

Walker placed his hand on the small of her back, and her skin tingled. How could his touch, or a simple look from him, get her heart racing so?

That was the reason she'd hesitated resigning. She'd given up her life for a man before, and look how that had turned out. She'd been praying, but hadn't heard from God yet. That meant wait, which was hard, but she'd obey.

The turmoil she'd felt while waiting on the answer had

been painful, but if this was where God wanted her, He wouldn't let her miss it.

"I'll wash," Cora said. "Trisha and Walker can dry. Ethan and Laney can put things away. Everyone else needs to leave the kitchen, pronto."

"Nope. No, I got that," Ethan said as he took the big soup pot out of Laney's hands.

"Sweetheart, I can put a pot away." Laney rolled her eyes at Trisha. "I'm not breakable." Then she and her husband shared a sweet kiss.

Ethan's gaze lingered on his wife. It was filled with such admiration that a twinge of jealousy came over Trisha. She'd always longed for a love like that.

When Walker handed her a towel, their fingers collided. The contact made her pulse kick. She tried to focus on drying the pan he'd handed her, but with every look and touch, she couldn't help but fall for him more and more.

That was why this decision about her career worried her. If she walked away from her life in academia, she might never get it back.

Before she knew it, her towel was soaked and the enjoyable stint of cleaning the kitchen was over. Now it was time to corral the kids and head home. She kind of liked how that sounded. The feeling in her belly at the thought of their nightly routine made her heady.

"This is a perfect night to go on a twilight UTV run around the property," Wade said. "Who wants to join me?"

Everyone stepped forward except Walker, who found her hand and tugged her back. She searched his face, but his attention remained on his father.

"Then we'll come back for a bonfire," Wade continued. "The slightly cooler weather tonight will be perfect for s'mores." All the children cheered.

"Trisha and I will stay behind," Walker said as he squeezed her hand. "We'll prep the bonfire."

Her stomach somersaulted at remaining with him. At his request, no less.

They followed the group onto the porch and then down the steps as the conversation turned to the slightly cooler weather and the possibility it meant rain was headed their way. Then the kids started announcing who they wanted to ride with.

Sophie, Tommy and Gabby rushed over. "Can we go on the ride without you, please?" Sophie pleaded for all three of them.

"Absolutely," Walker said as he ruffled Sophie's wavy hair. The three kids hugged him and then Trisha.

Trisha's eyes watered at how sweet the children were and how honored she was to help parent them.

She'd come to town with the plan to help Walker acclimate the children to living on a farm. Instead, she'd gained the family she'd never thought she wanted. Yes, she might return to Iowa, but no matter what happened with her and Walker, she knew she would be part of the children's lives forever.

Lord, I want to stay here. The horse farm and the children need me, and I adore Walker. Please guide me in what to do, but know that my heart is here.

She knew God could turn her heart toward returning to Iowa and resuming her life there. God had that power.

Walker slung his arm around her shoulders and pulled her closer as the first group took off. They waved until all three utility terrain vehicles were little specks.

The comfort of his powerful arm warmed her core. She'd never felt so accepted, so cared for, so acknowledged. Ever. Tears threatened, but she willed them away.

Right then, she noticed it. The worry she'd had about staying was gone. Completely.

God had granted her divine peace about staying here and resigning from Iowa State. Her heart leaped with the decision and images of her future in Serenity.

As the sun dipped low and the horizon turned numerous shades of orange and pink, she realized she was in love with Walker.

She tipped her head onto his shoulder. This was perfection. She could stand here with him forever.

He and Trisha walked hand in hand across the gravel parking lot, stones crunching beneath their footwear, cowboy boots for him, little tennis sneakers for her. It shocked Walker that he'd had the guts to pass on the UTV ride. Was the whole family wondering if he and Trisha had a romantic relationship? With his arm draped over her shoulder as the utility vehicles left, it was likely obvious to all.

"The nice thing about your mother's camp is that we get to use the amenities," Trisha said as she placed her other hand on his elbow.

She was so close, could she hear his heart pounding? He hoped not, because ever since they'd made up two days ago, he'd been questioning if she had romantic feelings for him. Her responses tonight solidified his belief that she liked him. He still couldn't believe he had laughed at her when she mentioned leaving her thriving academia career for the horse farm. Thankfully, they'd been able to come together and talk it out, and she'd accepted his heartfelt apology.

"Sure is," Walker replied. "But we also grew up having to tend to the upkeep of everything camp related, so it's a fair price to pay."

Trisha looked so different from when she'd arrived at the horse farm nearly two months ago. Her smooth skin was sun-kissed, highlighting her adorable freckles, and her thick hair had lightened to a gorgeous auburn color under the summer sun's intense rays. She rarely wore a cowboy hat, but when she did, her smoky emerald eyes let off a mysterious aura.

He led the way to the woodpile. "Why don't you have a seat? You've had a long day. I can gather the wood."

"No, I want to help." She took a few logs while he loaded as many as his arms could hold.

With her fashionable capri pants and fancy top, she wasn't dressed for work. More like luxury.

They dropped the logs near the sunken pit surrounded by rocks he and his brothers had collected on their property. "My brothers and I helped my dad build this, probably twenty years ago."

He stuck the tallest piece of wood into the ground and wiggled it so that it stood on its own, then settled the other pieces around it to form a tepee. "Our dad taught us how to build fires. This technique works well."

His stomach fluttered with the desire of stealing a kiss with Trisha tonight while everyone was off in the utility vehicles.

Yes, it was time. They'd danced around their feelings for a while now, and he wanted her to know how he felt. Those two weeks with her upset with him had been hard. He wanted to establish a "them" before they hit another snafu like that.

They wandered underneath a grove of trees to gather sticks for kindling.

"Growing up here must have been so amazing," she

said, placing a handful of sticks in the crate he was carrying.

He paused. "You know, it was. But at the moment, I'm not sure how much I enjoyed it." His mind was filled with all the negative talk from high school. How he'd believed his father didn't need him at the ranch, so he'd persuaded himself to go to school for something important. "And here I am, seriously thinking of leaving my cybersecurity career."

"So you're serious?"

"Serious as a heart attack." As his words slipped into the air, he felt more confident. "It's just the walking away from my corporate salary that's hard."

She dropped more sticks into his crate, then touched his elbow. "I know you'll make the best decision for everyone involved."

Her face held such trust. How could she be so confident when he was scared to walk away from the financial security? "I still can't believe you're thinking of leaving your life in academia."

A slow grin covered her face. "I'm staying," she stated, then rushed on to amend, "Assuming the horse show is a success, and how can it not be with an Olympian meet and greet?"

His heart skipped a beat at her admission. Yes, the kids needed her, and she was an amazing barn manager, but right now he could only think about Trisha as a woman, and a future with her.

She grinned, excitement sparkling in her exquisite eyes.

"That's great, Trisha. The kids are going to be excited."

"We need to pay off that ginormous vet bill first. Then we can tell them."

"Mum's the word, then." When she let out a little sigh, adrenaline flooded his system. Could they have a relationship? Now that she was staying, it was an actual possibility. "That should be enough kindling."

With her hand tucked in his, they headed back to the firepit, the crate of kindling wedged under his arm. He thanked God for opening his eyes and helping him forgive himself for the accident. That was all in the past, where he wanted it to stay.

In front of the firepit, he bunched up the sticks and twigs at the base of the wooden tepee he'd built. He took a match and lit the fire, watching the small flames lick the dry wood and grow.

A light breeze whispered through the trees and the comforting smell of burning wood lifted in the air. Trisha stood off to the side, as though unsure of what to do.

"Let's sit," he said. A variety of Adirondack chairs his parents had collected through the years surrounded the firepit. As the fire crackled, he led her to a double-wide chair and settled next to her. He put his arm along the back of the faded chair while his pulse skyrocketed with her nearness.

His old fear that something would happen to a loved one and they'd be harmed rose, but he pushed it away. He was a new man. He'd forgiven himself for the car accident that had never been his fault anyway, and now he was solidly leaning on God.

He dropped his arm around her shoulders and she snuggled close, as if she'd been made to fit into his arms. He breathed in a hint of her lightly scented floral soap or shampoo—he wasn't sure which.

The breeze picked up, reminding him the family would return soon. Should he really test out the notion of *them* and kiss her?

She turned. "Did you hear what Sophie said about loving her life in the country?"

"I did." Contentment swirled through him at Trisha's decision to stay and at how well the children were progressing. "Confirmation we made the right choice by going through with the purchase of the horse farm."

"I'm so happy for the kids. They are doing so well."

"Agreed."

"Do you really think Gabby is ready for preschool?" She picked up his hand and squeezed. "I mean, if we're both here, she can stay at the farm."

"She could, but we don't need to decide right now." The warmth of her hand made his senses spin.

"I don't know what I would do if all three of them went to school in the fall." Her face scrunched and a tear dropped off her eyelash.

He reached up and brushed his thumb across her soft cheek. He wanted to say something to comfort her, but with his touch, her worry about the children seemed to vanish. The cicada song fell to the background as his heart yearned for Trisha.

The air around them seemed electrified when he lowered his head and touched his lips to hers. She tasted like the sweet carrot cake they'd had for dessert.

He leaned back and cupped her face with his hands while a jumble of emotions rushed through him. He gazed into her mesmerizing green eyes as her face mirrored his attraction. Right then, he realized he had fallen completely and madly in love with Trisha. His heart hitched.

Love? The idea excited and scared him at the same time.

At the distant rumble of the UTVs returning, she looked toward the pastures.

When her gaze flitted back to him, he kissed her once more. He'd never thought he would love again, but here he was. Trusting her and their newfound relationship felt right.

"Let's go see the kids," Trisha said. Then she took his hand and headed toward the equipment shed where the vehicles would be parked.

The heat of her skin and the awareness that she seemed all in with this relationship told Walker he wasn't walking down this path alone.

But after the heartbreaking loss of Phoebe, keeping his fears at bay wasn't easy.

What would happen if he ended up nursing a broken heart again?

Chapter Thirteen

Early Friday morning in the upper barn, Trisha tossed a shovelful of wet sawdust into the gooey mound growing taller in the open trailer. Her throat constricted at the extra work someone's mistake had caused for them, but she was thankful because it could have been worse.

"That's it, boss," Buck said as Ryder drove the truck connected to the dump trailer full of wet sawdust out of the barn. He collected Trisha's and Walker's shovels. "I'll get a rake and smooth the gravel on the path."

"Thank you, Buck. You and Ryder have been a blessing this morning." Trisha wiped the dripping sweat off her face with a now-sodden washcloth as Buck nodded and ambled toward the path between the barns, rakes in hand. She stuck the damp fabric in her back pocket. "You too." She gave Walker a shy smile.

"I can't believe one of our boarders left the hose on overnight and created so much damage. That doesn't happen on a cattle ranch," Walker stated, his voice full of disappointment.

"And with the horse show tomorrow." She sighed and toed the deep divot the water stream had created in the hard dirt-patch corridor. "We were planning to give tours this weekend in the hopes of getting a couple more boarders to fill up our stalls. What are we going to do now?" She blinked away the tears that had sprung to her eyes.

He tugged her hand and pulled her into a hug. Her heart stuttered at the contact.

She buried her face in his strong chest, breathed him in and sank into the protected feeling. Long ago, she'd given up on her dream of true love, but apparently, God had not.

When Walker had kissed her two nights ago, she had been about to burst with happiness. The way he'd asked for permission with his eyes proved he was a gentleman.

"I'll work with Buck and Ryder to get some dirt on here," he said. "If I'm not mistaken, Archie has a tamper around here somewhere." He pressed a kiss to her forehead. "Don't worry—the tours will be just fine."

"Um, Walker," Buck interrupted.

Trisha jumped out of the embrace as Walker winked at her. She felt heat rise up her neck and turned to busy herself.

"Sorry about that," Buck said. "The tent people are here and asking for you."

After Walker left and her heart rate slowed, Buck and Ryder helped her spread fresh sawdust in the stalls and then bring the horses back from the pasture. Had the stable hands seen the embrace?

In their silence, her mind flew to the kiss from the other night at the firepit and what their relationship could be. It had turned from a necessary friendship into something much more satisfying. Full of trust and confidence.

Now that she'd decided to stay in Serenity, as long as they could keep the farm, they could explore the relationship to its fullest.

Trisha's heart was full because she had her dream job, was no longer just teaching it. Now she'd be in the children's lives every day for the foreseeable future, and she had Walker.

Thank You, God, for bringing a man into my life who believes in me and builds me up. Someone I can see a bright future with. She sighed in contentment.

She shook away the pleasant thoughts because she needed to focus. Today was their last chance to prepare for the two-day horse show this weekend. If she and Walker had planned properly, this show would solidly get them out of the red.

"Tish," Sophie squealed, Gabby on her heels. "Patches came to me. She knows my voice."

Trisha squatted and high-fived the girl. "You're going to be a good dog mommy."

"What about Daisey?" Gabby asked, teary-eyed. "All she does is sleep and eat. I don't think she likes me very much."

Trisha folded her hands around Gabby's little fists. "Does she cuddle into you when you hold her?"

"Yes."

"That proves she loves you," Trisha told her. "Maybe she's a little lazy today, and that's why Patches was moving around more."

"Yeah, maybe she's tired?" Gabby said. "Maybe she had a nightmare last night and needs a nap today."

"Maybe," Trisha agreed. It had been a while since Gabby's last nightmare. She thanked God for the little girl's forward progress.

Sophie took her sister's hand. "We'll go back after lunch and see if Daisey's still sleeping."

Gabby threw her arms around Trisha. "I love you," she whispered.

Trisha's heart lurched with her sentiment. "I love you too, Gabby. You too, Sophie." The girls hugged her so hard that they tumbled over in a heap, laughing.

They stood and Trisha brushed away the sawdust from their pretty clothes.

They'd matured so much since she'd arrived two months ago. No, they'd never forget or stop missing their parents, but they seemed like healthy young children, happy with the life they were now leading. Walker had been the right pick of guardian. He loved the children so much. Parker and Avery had made the perfect choice purchasing Serenity Stables for their children. Now so much was riding on the weekend.

"I'm going to brush Treasure," Sophie stated.

"Me too," Gabby said as she trailed after her sister toward the lower barn.

Trisha noticed Walker waving her over, so she made her way to him. She hoped the overnight barn flood was the only mishap today, but the dark clouds above made the promising day feel ominous. He tugged on the brim of his hat, highlighting the sparkle in his eyes.

"The tent can't go where you want because the land is too sloped," Walker said. "I was thinking over there?" He pointed to another spot she had been considering. Maybe not perfect, but it would do. People with dark green T-shirts were lugging over tent pieces. The one gentleman with his eye on Walker must be in charge.

"That works." She wrapped her hands around his upper arm. "What about the meet-and-greet tent for Kent?"

Walker gave the tent coordinator a thumbs-up and the workers began erecting the enormous tent. "They'll put it at the far end of the lower barn, so there will be space for the line of people waiting to get a picture with him."

"I'd love it if there were a line," she said, afraid to say anything else. So much depended on the success of tomorrow.

"You have the gift of organization, Trisha. You truly are the best barn manager around."

She grinned, relieved he wanted her to stay and still seemed interested in pursuing her, because she really liked him. Well, if she were honest, she loved him. The awareness settled deep in her chest. It felt good. Real good. The fear she'd known a few weeks ago was totally and completely gone.

She felt so free.

The tent person called to her, but before she could step away, Walker pulled her to him and whispered he'd miss her. His soft words made her pulse jump.

As she made her way over to the man with the hunter green polo and the tent company logo on his chest, all her failed relationships flashed in her mind. She had never lived up to anyone's expectations in the past. Was Walker any different? Her steps faltered.

Her judgment of men had always been off. Maybe she was wrong about Walker as well. Going back to Iowa was the safest thing, except she wanted to stay. Craved it, actually.

Her mind traveled to her memory verse for the week, about trusting the Lord with all her heart and not leaning on her own understanding. The perfect verse for right now. She was following God's lead here—she was sure of it.

Across the way, Walker caught her eye and placed his palms over his heart. Her stomach flip-flopped.

She answered all the tent questions and then stood back as the portable structure took shape.

"Did you hear?" Amanda sidled up to Trisha with a reluctant step.

She closed her eyes, bracing for whatever bad news Amanda held on her tongue. "What?" She gazed at their riding instructor, her cowboy hat sitting low on her forehead and her lower lip caught between her teeth.

"Weather people are still calling for rain and they've upped the percentages for Sunday."

Her heart sank at the unfortunate news. "Pray. It's all we can do."

Trisha scurried off to tell Walker the updated forecast.

He had his phone to his ear, but seemed to drink in her presence when she arrived. Chemistry sizzled between them.

She smiled at his attention. "What's going on?" she whispered and pointed to his phone.

"Bleacher people," he said. "I'm on hold."

She glanced at her watch and did a double take. They were late. Super late. She hoped there wasn't a problem.

"Yes, I'm still here." His face fell. "What do you mean you have next Saturday scheduled for our rental?" He turned away and kept talking, explaining about the horse show tomorrow and how next weekend was August, so he clearly couldn't have given them the wrong date.

He got off the phone. "You probably heard they got the date wrong. But they hope to deliver before sundown."

"Oh good." Relief coursed through her like water on a hot summer day.

"Except they aren't what we ordered." He turned his phone around to show her a picture.

Her breath hitched. "That's only four rows and no hand-rails."

"Apparently, portable bleachers of a certain height aren't required to have hand- or guardrails. Has something to do with how far the top bench is off the ground." He shrugged. "I figured it was better than nothing."

Dread coursed through her body.

On their flyers, they'd advertised stadium seating that was expected to accommodate five times the amount of people the pictured dinky bleachers would hold. What were they going to do?

Once the center pole was stabilized for the tent and it was all set up, vendors began moving their things in, a hum of activity Walker hoped would cause solid profits. Though Trisha had somehow fully leased out the newly purchased horses and had started a variety of new riding lessons, whether they could keep the horse farm lay in the meet and greet's success this weekend.

Walker took her hands in his. "Trisha, look at me. The bleachers will arrive." How'd he get so fortunate to find a woman so passionate about the one thing that connected him with the children? *Thank You, Lord.* He squeezed her hands, so happy to be doing life with her.

She grinned, leaned forward and touched her lips to his cheek. "Thank you," she said, then dropped her gaze as though embarrassed.

His heart jumped into his throat at the soft caress. The kiss they had shared while his family was touring the Triple C Ranch on the utility vehicles was never far from his mind these days. He kept replaying the sweet moment, as though on an endless loop. Where'd she get such soft lips from, anyway?

Then last night, when she'd leaned in for a lingering good-night kiss before she retired to her apartment, his chest had knocked so hard he could barely fall asleep.

So, this was love.

The announcer ambled over and asked where the sound system was being stored. His voice was deep and authoritative, his diction clear. He'd be perfect. Trisha led him over to the equipment shed.

Walker enjoyed being around her. She might be the sweetest person he knew, and she was a great mother figure for the children. His gaze roamed the numerous activities happening on the property. All Trisha's ideas. The tent. The various vendors. The announcer. Sticking to the outside ring. She was such a wise barn manager, he couldn't believe they had interviewed that Chase guy and the man had impressed Walker. Everyone was subpar compared to her, and she was gorgeous to boot.

If he looked back on the state he'd been in when Trisha had arrived in their lives, she had saved them. He'd been on the road to failure with the horse farm, never thinking he'd have to spend money to make money. Thankfully, God had brought Trisha into his life. Though keeping the farm was still an unknown, at least they were closer because of her.

A crackle resounded in the air as the announcer tested the sound system equipment.

Walker was thrilled she was staying on as barn manager, but a little piece of him always believed this wouldn't be enough for her and she'd leave. Would he love again and not be able to guard her from harm?

He halted his swirling thoughts. No, he was a new man. God had his back. He no longer had to protect his heart because God would lead the way, and right now he felt led to pursue Trisha.

"First in the ring." The announcer's deep voice filled the air as Autumn wandered over and stepped up beside him.

"The vendors will be an enormous hit," his sister said, gazing at the huge white tent. "I just saw a jewelry maker and got ankle bracelets for the girls with their puppy names on them."

"Autumn, you spoil them."

"Well, someone's got to."

The tent was no longer a huge white cavity, now that the vendors had moved their things inside and decorated their spaces. It looked inviting for shoppers to peruse. "This whole thing is for the kids, and if we can't become profitable, they may not be able to live here."

She bumped his shoulder. "You worry too much. Kent's going to be a huge success tomorrow. And with Trisha staying on as barn manager and you likely staying as well, you won't have to pay salaries, which is the biggest expense."

His jaw shifted. "Well, I won't have my corporate salary anymore."

"It'll work out. You're so much happier here than in your little computer world."

She was right, because he couldn't imagine leaving to settle on a computer eight hours a day for work again, no matter how much money he could make.

"Those dark clouds sure look ominous," she said.

Walker turned his attention to the fast-moving clouds in the sky. *Lord, if You see fit, please hold the rain off until Sunday evening.*

"Think it'll rain tomorrow?"

"I've been praying God would grant us two clear days. There have been enough mishaps for this show, and it isn't even noon." His stomach grumbled with a complaint. He sniffed popcorn from the vendors' tent. Were they selling it yet? He itched to find out.

"Do you smell that?" Trisha said as she joined the two. She lifted her nose in the air. "I love fresh-popped popcorn."

His pulse beat a staccato at her nearness. "Then stick close to me," Walker said as he wrapped an arm around Trisha and kissed the top of her head. "That's my next stop."

"Okay, enough lovey-dovey stuff. I'm outta here," Autumn said and turned to leave.

Lilly Bug charged right at Trisha. She opened her arms and the Jack Russell jumped into them. She snuggled Lilly Bug, who put her paws on Walker's chest and licked his face.

"Is this what Patches, Spot and Daisey will do soon?" Had he made a mistake letting each of the kids keep a puppy?

Trisha put a now-squirming Lilly Bug onto the ground. She raced off. "Calm down, Walker. You made the right decision letting them each have a pup. We live on a farm, for goodness' sake." She tipped her head into his shoulder and he thought he could just stand there all day long. "It'll be a wonderful bonding experience for them. You'll see."

"Sorry to be the bearer of bad news," Autumn said as she returned. "But Chestnut Street is now under construction."

"Oh no, the road that leads here," Trisha said.

"Is the town doing work on it?" Walker stepped toward the road, but there was no way to see the construction work from there.

"They're repaving it," Autumn stated. "They're detouring around, but it's a significant detour since there aren't many roads out this way."

Any other time, road construction would be a simple inconvenience. But they hoped to have tons of traffic coming their way tomorrow.

He rubbed the back of his neck and shot Trisha a supportive smile, but her lips were tense in worry.

"Walka," Gabby screamed as she ran to him, holding out her arm.

As Trisha gasped in surprise, he ate up the distance between them and lifted the girl in one fell swoop. "What's wrong, sweetie?" His heart jackhammered. Had she broken an arm, twisted an elbow, scraped a palm? She was so sweaty and disheveled, he couldn't tell.

"I huwt my fingew," she wailed, tears streaming down her face.

Thankfully, her arm, elbow, wrist, palm and fingers looked fine. "Which one?" Trisha had moved beside them, her head leaning over his shoulder.

Gabby shoved her index finger at him, her sobs turning into little hiccups.

He pressed a kiss on the pad of her finger, and relief seized him. "There, all better." He'd seen Laney, his sister-in-law, doing this with her twins, and somehow it made the child forget all about the boo-boo. He tenderly palmed the tears away from Gabby's cheek, fully aware of Trisha's closeness and how this parenting moment felt so good.

In answer, Gabby snuggled her little head into his shoulder and stuck her thumb in her mouth, which she did when she was tired. Maybe they'd have to put her down for a nap.

"We were just headed to get some popcorn. Hungry?"

She straightened. "Yes." Her head swiveled as she looked around, probably unaware that popcorn had been popping.

He took Trisha's hand in his and they wove through the vendors, eyes peeled for the glass cabinet with *Popcorn* written in red on the side and a luscious treat lying within.

As they passed a stall, he heard someone speaking. "Sure, the registered participants will come because they already paid, but will the public put in the extra effort with all that road construction?"

He slid a glance at Trisha and her eyes widened.

"They'll show up, right?" she whispered.

"I'm sure they'll come," he replied, but the vendor had a point. They might not.

If they didn't have a superb turnout, Kent's meet and greet wouldn't be the success they'd hoped for.

As he brushed past a group of people, popcorn in sight, he broke out in a cold sweat. What if they had to sell?

What would happen to the children then?

Chapter Fourteen

Late that night, Trisha's weather app woke her with a severe storm watch notification. She bolted up in bed and tapped the radar icon to see a large red blob headed their way. Oh no!

She hurriedly got dressed. They had been expecting possible rain, but not a severe storm. When had this popped up and how long would it last?

Worry settled in her gut as a vision of tomorrow's horse show failing skittered across her mind. When she opened her apartment door, the wind fought to steal it from her. As she battled and won, rain sprinkles peppered her face. She rushed down the steps right as Walker charged across the gravel drive in the darkness, both of them likely planning to check on the horses and button up the property before the red blob hit.

Autumn had agreed to sleep over since Trisha and Walker both needed to get an early start in the morning for the horse show. At least the kids were safe in the house with her.

"Where did this storm come from?" Walker asked as he pulled the hood of his bright yellow rain jacket over his head. A wind gust grabbed his unsecured baseball cap and it went flying. He let it tumble away and focused on tightening his hood instead.

"I don't know, Walker, but it's only a watch, so we have time to check the horses."

Walker clasped her hand and she gazed up at the sweet tenderness on his face. She felt his love for her right down to her toes.

Heat radiated from his hand to hers. She felt so complete beside him that suddenly this storm didn't seem so severe.

"Buck texted. He's on his way to check the horses and verify all the barn doors are latched tight," Walker replied. "I need to move the PA system inside and check the tent, since we weren't expecting weather like this."

She nodded. "I can help, but I can't lift that heavy PA system." Thankfully, they'd had the foresight to cover the speakers with plastic bags earlier, but the PA equipment was open to the elements.

"No problem," he yelled as the rain grew heavier and louder. He squeezed her hand and let it drop, and then they rushed toward the outdoor arena. "I'll move the system inside and you can check the tent."

What neither of them voiced was their concern over the fate of the horse show and the meet and greet. Would this storm ruin their chances of saving the farm? Trisha pushed the negative thoughts out of her head. They had work to do and worry wouldn't help.

Buck pulled into the lot, gave a quick wave and then ran to the upper barn.

As she and Walker dashed over the gravel, rain pelted her face. She had a good feeling about her and Walker.

They were going to make it—she just knew it. He was such a good leader and they had laid a solid foundation.

Right then, the wind picked up and rain began to fall in sheets. Both their phones beeped with a notification that they were now under a warning.

Worried, she stopped and studied her phone. "Should we take cover?" The storm became angrier as a sharp wind whipped around them and fat raindrops pummeled their faces.

He waved her forward. "We'll just take care of these quick items and meet back in the house, okay?" He cupped her wet cheek. "Stay safe," he said, then turned and raced to the soaking PA equipment.

Trisha felt uneasy about ignoring the app's recommendation to find a safe place to shelter, but Walker had lived here his whole life. He'd know if they were in danger or not.

Anyway, this was all her fault. She shook her head at her own ignorance as she jogged to the tent. What had she been thinking pushing the show to be outdoors when they could have had an indoor event? Yesterday afternoon she could have switched course and officially moved the show indoors. But no, she had been stubborn, greedy. She had wanted as many people as possible to show up, and their indoor viewing capacity was super limited.

After she ducked into the massive tent, she went about checking each of the pole connections. She needed to stop stressing because, within a few minutes, they'd all be safe indoors. She prayed for the rain to end and the ground to dry so they'd be able to host the horse show, and Kent's meet and greet would be successful enough to save the farm.

Time was running out and this was their final chance.

* * *

The wind howled and rain plastered Walker's jacket against his body. He could barely see in front of him as he rushed back to gather the last part of the PA system and lug it into the safety of the dry barn.

A crack sounded, drawing his attention to the massive oak right next to the tent. As the tree began to lean, a vise tightened around his chest.

"No," he shouted, though it came out more like a choked utterance. Trisha was under that tent, checking the poles like he'd asked. Had she heard the crack? Would she find her way to safety? *Please, God.*

Adrenaline flooded his system as he charged around the ring, on his way to save the woman he loved dearly. The tree started an unhurried fall. The moment happened in painful slow motion while he moved as fast as he could.

With each step he took, the momentum of the gigantic tree picked up pace. As the great oak thudded to the ground, an invisible fist squeezed the breath from his lungs. The center of the tent crushed, the canvas ripped, poles flung as though they were toothpicks. Cracked tree limbs broke off and flew in the air, landing all over. But Trisha's safety was all he cared about. He raced as quickly as he could to the mangled tent.

Visions from the car accident floated in his head, the glint of metal the moment before the tragic impact, except he had been too late to react. If he had only seen the rig earlier, he could have swerved. Instead, the 18-wheeler had slammed into them.

His throat constricted at the perilous situation of the downed tree, but he rushed over to the most open part of the collapsed tent, praying for Trisha's safety.

Right then, the downed tree, which seemed to cover

the smashed tent entirely, rolled a few feet and then seemed to settle deeper into the earth.

He spotted her boots right away and lifted the thick canvas off Trisha, thankful nothing had pinned her. Though the tree and tent poles had spared her, blood ran down the side of her face from a nasty gash on her temple. She lay completely still, her features contorted, as though in pain.

Immediately he pressed two fingers onto her neck and felt for a pulse. *Thank You, Lord.*

"Wow, that happened fast," Buck said as he ran over and pushed his phone to his ear, rain still slamming down. "She unconscious?" At Walker's nod, Buck informed the emergency operator they needed an ambulance and explained what had happened.

Walker's stomach coiled into a tight knot, and he backed up. The scene was reminiscent of his wife after the fatal car accident. Back then, Walker had been helpless to do a thing, yet he could have saved her had he been paying closer attention prior to the crash. He knew he could have. If only he had somehow noticed the semi careening for them.

His pulse raced at the scene before him. This calamity could have been prevented if Walker had insisted Trisha head inside to safety when they'd met on the gravel drive. Or, at least, when the watch had turned into a warning. Why had he let her help? Especially after the app advised them to take cover.

All the blood drained from his head and dark speckles danced before his eyes. This was all his fault.

Trisha hadn't moved an iota since the tree had come down. That was bad, really bad. She couldn't die. She just couldn't. The kids adored her, and he loved her so much.

To have two deaths on his conscience would be unbearable.

He could feel Buck near him, heard him explain everything to the operator: the tree, the tent, Trisha, the gash at her temple, the blood dripping down her face. All Walker's fault.

Seconds turned into minutes. When would the ambulance arrive?

"Walker," Trisha whispered as she moved and then groaned.

He dropped to his knees and reached for her hand. His own reckless actions had put her in danger. Hadn't he learned anything from the past?

Trisha partially opened her fear-filled eyes. "What happened?" A siren sounded, followed by the sound of gravel spewing as an emergency vehicle arrived.

Panic thrummed through him while he stroked the back of her hand.

"A tree fell on the tent." She should be inside with the kids right now, safe and taking cover, just like responsible people did when storm warnings sounded. If only he'd done the right thing when the app had alerted them.

Emergency personnel hurried over. Walker quickly told them how long Trisha had been unconscious and then stepped away so they could do their job. The scene gutted him as his throat clogged with grief.

He'd done enough. More than enough. This was all his fault. The woman he cared about—loved—was hurt because of him.

Why had he let her help? Because he'd liked the way Trisha had looked at him when he'd taken charge tonight, that was why. He hadn't wanted to see her disappointed expression if he'd told her to go inside.

What a fool he'd been.

A lump clogged his throat and refused to budge. He'd been right. He never should have allowed himself to become involved with Trisha. His fear that he would love again and be unable to protect her had come true. *Way to go, Walker.*

More sirens wailed in the distance.

Something inside him shriveled, knowing those sirens were because of him. Again.

He should have known better. He had known better. Why had he let his guard down?

His insides twisted at the mess he'd made of today and at the pain he'd caused his loved ones.

Lord, please don't let Trisha die because of my carelessness.

The tiny waiting room spilled over with family and friends, and Walker's head pounded at the events of the past few hours. All he could do was pace. The doctor had just given them an update on Trisha—grade four concussion and some painful bruising. She'd been moved to a regular room for overnight observation and could be visited. He refused.

He roughed a hand over his face. He couldn't see her damaged like that, not knowing it was all his fault.

So, Autumn had visited first. Ethan and Laney had just left to spell his sister.

His mother was at the horse farm with the children and the storm had passed. Though he hadn't talked with anyone about the show status, he assumed the downed tree and collapsed tent hadn't halted the events of today since they had an indoor arena.

Beeping sounded in the distance and his stomach

turned at the smell of industrial cleaner clinging to the air. Just like that awful night six years ago.

"I just got a text from your mom," Wilbur stated from his spot, leaning against the sterile concrete wall as Walker passed him for the umpteenth time. "The kids are awake and doing just fine."

He was such a calming force, and since the older man knew Walker's entire messy background, he could guess what was filtering through his mind.

Walker thanked him and kept going.

Autumn strode over and poked her finger in his chest. "She wants to see you," she growled. "What is it with you? This is not like Phoebe. Trisha will be just fine."

"It was all my fault," he mumbled. He'd been thinking it nonstop, like a mantra, ever since the moment he'd seen the massive tree crush the tent. There was no way he could face Trisha and see her bruises, knowing she was in pain because of him. No way.

Regret clawed at him and he welcomed it.

His sister pinned him against the corner with her index finger and her blazing eyes. He felt like a caged lion.

"It's not your fault," Autumn said, removing her pointer from his chest. "She asked to help. It was an accident."

Is she kidding me? His sister was so naive. She'd never been through a hardship in her life. How dare she try to counsel him?

"Come on, Autumn. It's *all* my fault. I sent her under that tent. Me, stupid me."

"She wanted to help, ya know. She would not have taken no for an answer." She flashed him an angry look.

He shook his head. "My fault."

She leaned back. "Don't you believe God is in control? Don't you believe He has a plan?"

Her words rocked his world. Yes, he believed what she said, but walking by faith was too hard. Living inside his little shell was easier.

Autumn threw up her hands in disgust, then turned and strode away.

He didn't care whether he annoyed his sister, because he'd made a pact with himself after Phoebe's death. He'd had his chance at love and he'd failed. Period.

His chest gave a tight squeeze. Why in the world had he allowed Trisha into his heart? He'd had true love once. When had he become so greedy? He wasn't sure why in the world he had been playing with fire by allowing love into his life again.

The foolishness had to stop. Now.

He'd already failed one woman. Sure, Trisha had made it out alive this time, but what about the next? He didn't want something even worse happening to her because of him. She didn't deserve it.

The least he could do was protect her from his incredibly poor choices.

In the mostly deserted hallway, he looked at his phone. The wallpaper was a photo of the five of them the day they'd picnicked at the lake. An ache pressed in on his heart. He'd miss playing family with her, but this had to stop or someone would get hurt again, and next time, it might be fatal.

He had no choice but to put distance between himself and Trisha.

"I just got a text that the committee canceled the show because of all the downed trees over roads and local flooding," Wilbur stated. Then he put his hand on Walker's shoulder. "Even though Serenity Stables has an indoor arena, it's too dangerous for people to travel to the show."

Walker's stomach bottomed out at the news. What Wilbur didn't say was that it was over. No horse show. No successful meet and greet. They no longer had any choice in the matter; they'd have to sell the horse farm.

"Not sure that you know, though Trisha does, but these shows are scheduled well in advance. When one is canceled because of weather, they either tack it onto the end of the season or combine the points from other shows."

He nodded his thanks to the older man. Trisha had already told him about their cancellation policy. They couldn't wait three months for the meet and greet to happen.

All was lost. They had failed the children.

In one moment, he'd lost Trisha and the horse farm.

He closed his eyes and pushed the verse about walking by faith out of his head, especially the mention of courage in the very next verse.

He'd have to tell Trisha about their failure and make it clear there was no *them* anymore.

It would hurt now, but in the long run, it was the very best thing for Trisha, and that was all he cared about. One day, she'd even thank him.

He could never forgive himself for the damage he'd done today. He knew, no matter what platitudes came out of her mouth, that she'd never forgive him for his thoughtless actions and the pain he'd caused her.

When Walker entered the room, Trisha's heart stuttered. She smiled, but an excruciating pain shot to her head at the action. She pressed her lips together and closed her eyes against the bright lights. *Thank you, grade four concussion.*

The antiseptic scent she'd smelled since arriving yesterday wafted in with him and turned her stomach.

She'd been waiting to be reunited with Walker since the moment the rescue team had arrived last night and he had stepped away. She had missed him during the ambulance ride. While they had wheeled her from one place to another on a stretcher, a sweet nurse had placed a cool towel across her eyes to mask the painful light. Once she'd arrived in the hospital room, she'd wondered where he'd been. Why hadn't he come to see her? She just wanted his presence, his comfort, his love.

Hopefully, the doctors would sign her release papers soon so they could go home. The beeping from the machines had been driving her crazy. Every beep sliced into her temple and made her head pound even harder. She missed the kids and the farm, but mostly Walker.

Every person who'd come in to visit had told her he'd be right in. They'd assured her the children were fine and at home with Cora. So where had Walker been since yesterday morning? It had been over twenty-four hours since the tree had fallen on the tent, and she needed him by her side.

Last night, she'd wept when visiting hours had ended and he hadn't shown, but the medication they'd had her on made her drowsy and she'd fallen into a fitful sleep. With nurses waking her every hour to make sure she was okay, it elated her to finally see him.

"Hey," she whispered. He wore the same clothing he'd had on during the storm. The scruff on his chin was longer and his hair was mussed, like maybe he'd slept in the waiting room last night. If he'd been there, why hadn't he come into her room?

She held out her hand, but he didn't take it. Maybe she'd imagined his arrival. She squinted. Sure enough, he stood at the end of her bed, hands gripping the railing, eyebrows furrowed.

"What's wrong? Is it one of the kids?" Fear shot through her body as she tried to sit up and failed.

Frown in place, he moved to her bedside. His arms tightly crossed in front of his chest. "The kids are fine. My mother is staying with them." He smiled, though it appeared pained.

Her fear subsided. A little. "What's wrong, then?"

He gazed at the ceiling as though praying. What in the world was wrong?

"Listen, Trisha. I'm sorry." His gaze flitted around the room and landed somewhere beyond her bed. "I understand how you feel. I'm upset with myself as well." His gaze sharpened on her, but his eyes were flat. Unemotional.

Before she could question him and ask what he was talking about, he drew in a tight, audible breath, then spoke.

"The committee called off the show," he said, lifting his chin. "No show, no meet and greet. We have to sell." Walker shoved his fingers in his front pockets, then pulled them out and rubbed his hands in front of him as though he was unsure what to do with himself.

"We can't sell! Maybe we could—"

"It's over, Trisha. We don't have a choice."

No show? She pressed her eyes tight and held back the tears that threatened. They'd failed. The kids would lose the place where their parents had wanted them to be raised. Worse yet, they'd have to sell to that housing developer.

All she wanted was to hold his hand. Have him comfort her after that scary accident. Why was he acting so distant?

"I'll go back to my cybersecurity job and you'll return to Iowa, just like we planned."

"No." Her sharp word ricocheted around the space like an out-of-control ball in a small racquetball room. "Maybe I can get a job around here. I don't want to leave…the kids." *Or you.*

The children. How would they tell them they'd have to move again? That they couldn't stay in their new home, the place they'd grown to love.

Walker tightened his jaw. "You can come back to visit on holidays. The kids would like that."

She shook out the confusing cobwebs from the concussion as she processed that he was pushing her away. His words gutted her. Was he breaking up with her?

Her mouth opened. She probably looked like a guppy drawing in air. He hadn't come to comfort or to calm her. He'd come to inform her they were selling and she was no longer needed. How could she leave him? The kids?

Apparently, he'd been using her all this time to salvage the horse farm because of her equine skills. Her heart cracked open at his callous behavior.

He took a small step away from the bed, creating even more distance between them. Their gazes clashed across the small space and his eyes filled with something. Sorrow? No. She gave a mental shake of her head. More like relief that he could finally move on with his corporate life. Without her.

"We'll contact the lawyer this week. Have him let Silver Developers know we're ready to sell."

She gave him one somber nod. They didn't have a

choice. How would the children take the loss of the horse farm and home they'd come to love?

Walker's cold reaction to losing the farm caused the fine hairs on her arms to rise. Why had she thought they were a thing? At the first hint of trouble, Walker ran away. She'd never been good enough for a McCaw.

Panic crawled up the back of her throat, but she swallowed it. She had known better than to fall in love and let her guard down.

Though she still had her life in Iowa, that wasn't where her heart was. She wanted to stay here—Serenity had become like home to her. For the first time, she felt like she belonged. Was loved.

Boy, had she been misguided.

She looked away and closed her eyes against the threatening tears. He didn't want her. Righteous anger bubbled up from deep within. She could have written the end to this short-lived love story—it seemed the theme of her heart-wrenching life.

"I think it best that you return to Iowa." His Adam's apple bobbed with emotion. "You have a booming career there." He left the words *and now you can go back to that life* unsaid.

He didn't want her.

Most likely had never loved her.

But the kids… She couldn't leave Sophie, Tommy and Gabby. She couldn't.

She willed the tears to stay at bay, lifted her chin and stared into his emotionless eyes.

"I told you I wanted to stay. Permanently." She shot him a glare that stabbed pain from her eyeballs to the back of her head. All Trisha wanted was family, but all she'd ever experienced was rejection. She'd thought this time it would be different.

He gave her a tiny shake of his head. Such a resounding *no*, it felt like he had screamed it. He wanted her out of his life and was throwing her away like yesterday's trash. For good.

She'd been wrong. Oh, so wrong.

She'd never been good enough for true love to stick around, and this situation was no different.

He was right—she should go back to Iowa. Pick up where she'd left off. Try to forget the best two months of her life.

Her excitement about seeing Walker had vanished. The thought of sitting the children down to let them know they'd failed. Well, she simply couldn't take all this pain right now.

"I'm exhausted."

"I'll leave you to rest."

The door clicked shut behind him, and it was over. The dream of being loved and cherished, a true McCaw, raising their little family together as a team, finally stepping into a perfect career.

And the farm. They'd disappointed the children miserably. How had that happened so quickly?

Yes, in the back of her mind, she had always known he'd leave her. Except, she hadn't thought it'd be so quick and so painful. Now her heart ached more than her head.

She felt used. Worthless.

She twisted her college ring. She should have known it wouldn't last, that she wasn't good enough for love to endure. She'd known it before she'd arrived in Serenity, and Walker's actions today had confirmed her beliefs.

Those annoying tears she'd been fighting while he'd

been in the room streaked down her face and onto the bedding. She didn't even try to blink them away.

Why, God? Why? Why would You bring Walker into my life and allow me to fall so desperately in love, only to have him trample my heart and walk away? And why did You give us such hope with the horse show, only to crush the children's dream?

She hadn't been worthy enough for her father to make her a priority. For the two men she had loved to stay.

And now Walker. She'd never been worthy enough for him.

She should have known better than to fall in love. To trust. To hope.

Because in the blink of an eye, it was all over.

Chapter Fifteen

It had been four days since he'd caused Trisha's grade four concussion and subsequently had the final heart-breaking conversation with her. Sure, she'd been arriving at dawn to watch the children while Walker did morning chores at the barns, but she'd also been ignoring his presence and leaving as soon as the kids were back in his care. Autumn had told him the concussion was getting better, but noise and light still bothered her.

When he finished his Tuesday-morning chores, he gazed at the brilliant blue sky. What was he gonna do without her?

He rubbed a hand over his face. Maybe he should be more worried about what the kids were going to do without this place? He and Trisha had to tell them and he needed to call the lawyer, but so far he hadn't had the guts to tackle either. He turned and walked through the upper barn, the neighing lifting his spirits.

Wilbur was leaning against the outside of the barn, a piece of straw sticking out of his mouth.

As Walker joined him, his mouth dropped open in shock at what he saw.

A tree company was cutting and hauling tree pieces away. Townspeople were picking up debris and fixing broken fence lines. The small bleachers were being replaced with the stadium version they'd originally ordered.

"What's going on?"

"We live in a small community, Walker. People help others."

"But everyone has storm damage to clean up from, not just us."

Wilbur shook his head as though Walker was dense. "Accept the help. The town loves you, Trisha and the kids, and they want to help."

Right then, Trisha walked out of the house, but instead of going to her Jeep, she came over to Wilbur, who gave her a long and gentle hug. When she asked the same questions and received the same responses, Trisha nodded, not seeming surprised at all.

Her eyes were dull and Walker wasn't sure if that was from the concussion, the breakup or losing the farm. Either way, his heart broke for her.

She started to walk away.

"I have something for both of you to hear," Wilbur said.

Trisha turned but made a point not to make eye contact with Walker.

"I contacted the committee folks, and they agreed to reschedule your show to this upcoming weekend."

Trisha sucked in a breath. "But what about the scheduled hosts for the weekend?"

"They've graciously allowed their venue to be rescheduled for the end of October."

"Wow."

Her one word summed up his feelings as well. He

glanced at her and noticed a single tear trickle down her cheek.

"Well, Chief, that is sweet, but the show itself won't save the horse farm, and I know for a fact Kent's only free weekend was this past one. Without Kent and the meet and greet, it's over." She wiped away the errant tear. "My head hurts. I'm going to lie down." Her face drawn, she turned and stalked away, the defeat in her tone piercing Walker to the core.

She had every right to feel defeated. They had not only lost each other, but had failed the children and had been unable to save the place where Parker and Avery had wanted them to grow up.

"Why don't you go after her?" the older man asked.

"She's going back to Iowa." At least, he assumed she was. "She's a big-time college professor there." That was a whole other world she belonged to that didn't include him. One that would accept her back with open arms and wouldn't hurt her like he had. She'd be safely cocooned in her academia life.

Walker refused to look at Wilbur. The older man had been telling him just that—work things out—since Sunday.

Wilbur cleared his throat. "Love rarely comes around—"

"Twice in a lifetime. I know," he interjected. "She was pretty perfect." Her green eyes always drew him in, didn't matter what she was talking about. She listened to him, heard him, and boy, was she a good problem solver. His heart sped up just thinking of her amazing character.

"Was? She's living at your mother's," Wilbur said in a miffed tone. "Go after her and right whatever wrong you made."

Walker wished he could. He missed Trisha and her

steady presence, her smart mind, her warm hand to hold. He never should have panicked and severed ties with her. Why had he done that?

Fear.

The same fear that had stopped him from living these past six years.

Hadn't he worked this out with God a few weeks ago and come out the other side a new man? He had put all his trust in Jesus, no longer living on his own.

What had happened to that new commitment?

"Walking by faith, not sight, is hard work," Walker stated, the words swirling through his mind.

"But God gives us the courage to do just that," Wilbur noted. "Did you even pray about your decision to break ties with Trisha?" Wilbur didn't wait for an answer, just ambled over to the riding ring.

Walker sucked in a breath. He hadn't prayed about it. Hadn't even thought to pray. He'd just done the one thing he'd thought would fix everything—end things with Trisha so he couldn't hurt her anymore.

He dropped his head to his hands. He had messed up by breaking things off with Trisha without planning it through and, as Wilbur had so eloquently hit spot-on, praying over it.

Right there, he poured his heart out to God while half the town worked at readying the farm for their upcoming event. He asked for forgiveness and direction and a chance to make it right. And for peace over the scary events of the storm that reminded him so much of the fatal car wreck six years ago.

After a long while, he lifted his head, his cheeks damp with the revelation to call Kent. Who knew? Maybe the

Olympian was free this weekend? With God, anything was possible.

He brought up his phone app and placed the call. After he explained they were in grave danger of losing the horse farm, he pleaded with Kent, as a personal favor to Trisha, to come this weekend for the rescheduled show so they could host the meet and greet.

"I'd be happy to, Walker. Your horse farm means a lot to me. Local stables are where kids experience horseback riding for the first time. I was young once and know it's where dreams are made." Kent released a breath, as though this topic made him emotional. "I'll do anything in my power to assure Serenity Stables stays around for a long time." He promised to contact his manager to work out his schedule and to send a text confirmation when his travel was booked.

Walker thanked him for his willingness to help and disconnected.

Without extensive advertising like they'd done for the previous event, this weekend might not bring in the money they had hoped. Either way, he wanted a shot at a relationship with Trisha.

Now Walker needed to seize the opportunity to apologize, bare his soul to her and, if she'd have him, make things right with her.

Because that day in the hospital, a part of him had been ripped away and he'd felt like the walking wounded ever since.

He now knew that living without her was worse than not being able to protect her. Way worse.

"Cora, what are you doing up so early?" Trisha asked the next morning when she entered the homey kitchen.

She'd been grateful Walker's mom had been willing to take her in until she got better from her concussion and could return to Iowa. Though, the more Trisha mulled Iowa over in her mind, the less she wanted to go back.

No matter what was going on with her and Walker, she couldn't leave the kids. The thought of returning to Iowa, after a taste of mothering these children and being a part of a horse farm again, just about tore her in two. She poured a mug of coffee and settled next to the older woman on the bench seat under the bay window.

"I live on a cattle ranch, sweetheart. I'm always up early." Cora sipped her black coffee. "But I'm usually in the bedroom since Wade set up a nice little coffee-and-tea station in the corner of our room. I love to spend a few hours in the Bible and praying, but I need my caffeine." She raised her worn Triple C Ranch mug for effect.

"Of course." Now that she thought about it, she'd usually heard Cora moving about as she was getting herself up this past week. Had it only been a few days since Walker had broken her heart?

She looked out the wide window, and the nighttime sky greeted her. In a few minutes, the black would turn into a color show of blushed oranges, pinks and blues, before the pretty glow would fade and the sun would rise.

"Walker's expecting me." Except she was not motivated to get in her Jeep and drive the couple of miles to the horse farm.

Could she stay in Serenity after selling Serenity Stables and with things between them so broken? She wasn't sure.

How could she live in this little town, run into him and pretend she didn't love him? Pretend she didn't want to be part of his future. Pretend she didn't want to be by his side forever.

Her heart squeezed in dread. She couldn't stay as much as she *had* to stay—for the kids, so she could be a part of their lives. Somehow, those three rascals had wound their way into her heart and she simply couldn't leave them. Even if Walker didn't want her.

Cora patted her hand. "It'll work out." When their gazes met, Trisha knew the older woman recognized exactly where her thoughts were running.

Trisha couldn't help that she wore her heart on her sleeve.

"Everyone knows hosting the horse show won't save the farm, right?"

"The townspeople wanted to do what they could to help."

"Without Kent's meet and greet, there's no hope. We have to sell. We don't have a choice."

"Just keep leaning on God. He has you." Cora kissed her cheek and retired to her room.

She was right. God was good. This summer, Trisha had learned to lean on Him all over again. The verse from Proverbs popped into her mind, about trusting the Lord with all your heart and not leaning on your own understanding. She trusted God to do His will in this matter. After the past eight spiritually dry years, she didn't want to go before Him and step out of His will. She would trust that if Walker was the man for her, then God would reunite them in His own timing.

And if not? Well, she had her Heavenly Father and the McCaw clan who had not walked away from her like Walker had.

As dawn's color show began and the brief time of

blushed oranges, pinks and blues showed themselves through the billowy clouds, a peace settled over Trisha and traveled down to her toes. Yes, having her fiancé dump her right before the wedding had been horribly painful, but the situation with Walker had been different. Yes, she loved him, but now she had the kids to consider. This summer she'd grown so much closer with her Lord. She'd become a mother figure to Sophie, Tommy and Gabby. She'd seen the children flourish while living in the home their parents had dreamed for them.

No, she wouldn't take a moment of this summer back, because too much good had happened. If she and Walker weren't meant to be, her heart would eventually mend. God would make sure of it. Yes, it might be painful and lengthy but, over time, she'd be able to move on. She and Walker were forever joined at the hip because of the kids, so somehow they'd have to mend fences. Except there was no way she'd let their nonstarter relationship affect the children. They deserved more from her and Walker.

She washed out her mug and then drove over to the horse farm, determined not to look at Walker's face, especially those captivating eyes she hadn't seen since the horrible day in the hospital. Since the day he'd broken her heart. Yesterday morning, he had touched her elbow to get her attention and she'd ignored him. She'd kept moving and hadn't looked back. Well, she'd actually sneaked a glance and spotted him tugging on his barn boots and leaving in what appeared to be a huff.

She parked and stepped out of her Jeep. Yes, she was glad he "broke up" with her, because she'd been wrong to pin her hopes on a man.

The door flew open and Walker rushed out. "Have you seen her?" he asked, his gaze roaming the property in the dawn's light. His already haggard face also held a worried look.

Unease clawed at her. "What's going on?" When their eyes met, Trisha refused to give in to the strong emotional pull.

He'd dumped her. For the kids' sake, they'd somehow have to find a new normal.

"Sophie is missing!"

Her pulse stuttered as she tried to take in the situation. "How?"

"Last night she wanted to go to the pond for a picnic and I refused. The day had been so busy with the town helping and the tree removal and the tent activity..." He dragged a hand through his hair. "She stomped off to her room without eating dinner and turned her back to me during story time. Wouldn't let me kiss her good-night." A tear edged his eyelash.

Trisha took his hands in hers, ignoring the tingle she felt from his touch. "Have you searched the entire house?" In her mind, she inventoried the house. There were no hiding spots the kids knew about that she and Walker didn't. Two months of playing hide-and-seek had taught her that.

"I did."

"Then she's at the pond." Because Sophie was one stubborn girl.

"No, that's too far. She knows she's not supposed to go there without us."

"Walker, she's a kid. Kids misbehave. Trust me, she's at the pond."

He gave her a hopeful nod and turned to the barn. "Let's ask Buck to wait in the house in case the others wake up while we're gone." She ran after him.

After Buck had headed for the house, they rushed through the barn to the equipment shed where the UTVs were kept.

In the morning's stillness, Trisha heard a soft noise before they exited the barn. She stopped and it sounded again.

Walker came over to her. "What?" he whispered.

She pointed at Treasure's stall and his eyes widened.

Sure enough, Sophie sat in the corner of the horse stall, holding her pony's head to her chest. The girl was covered in sawdust, and dirty tear streaks covered her cheeks. Trisha's heart sighed in relief.

She rushed to the girl's side. "Sweetie, what's going on?"

Sophie grabbed her and clung tight. "Don't leave. Walka won't smell the roses without you."

Trisha looked at Walker. He had his hand clamped around the back of his neck, a pained expression on his face.

What had started as a jab to get Walker to experience life had made a little girl sleep in the barn with her pony. Trisha felt horrible. This was all her fault.

"Sophie, I'm so sorry—"

"I am too," Walker interrupted. "I wish I had taken a moment and thought about your request. But, honey, leaving the house at seven years old without telling anyone is not okay."

Sophie sucked in a breath, her watery eyes showing a level of respect for Walker that Trisha hadn't yet seen.

An unfamiliar ache started in Trisha's chest, right next to the wound that had been ripped open last Sunday. She wasn't sure just how she was going to be in such close proximity to Walker day after day. This would be more excruciating than she'd thought.

He knelt down in front of them and gazed into Sophie's face. "Two wrongs don't make a right. Do you understand?"

The girl nodded and then lunged at Walker, who hugged her right back.

"Wanna go to the house? I could make pancakes," he offered.

"Only if Tish makes them," the smart girl said. Tears welled up behind Trisha's eyes, thankful they'd found her and everything was right in their little world. Or as right as it could get.

They each took her hand and walked out of Treasure's stall together. "How come you guys don't kiss and make up?" Sophie asked.

Heat flamed Trisha's cheeks at the youngster's words. How embarrassing. She flashed a glance at Walker and what she saw took her breath away. Was he just concerned for the children or had something changed between the two of them?

"There will be no kissing and making up until I grovel and apologize," Walker stated. His smoldering eyes never wavered from hers.

Butterflies took flight in her tummy. Was this the second chance she'd been praying for? If so, could she be strong enough to stay?

Yes. She could. If she got another chance with Walker, she'd grab hold and never let go. Ever.

The moment hung in the air long enough for Trisha to realize she didn't want any spectators there for what she hoped Walker was about to say.

"Listen, Sophie. How about you go along to the house?"

Trisha asked. "Buck is there, and he needs to get back to feed the horses. I'll be home in a couple of minutes." She gave Sophie a knowing glance and a slight nod.

Sophie's face transformed from upset to gleeful in a moment. "Yes, Tish, I'll do that." She hugged Trisha and then Walker. "As soon as you get back, I want to hear everything."

Trisha nodded as Sophie raced out of the barn, and she felt a whisper touch on her fingers as Walker took her hand.

"I am so very sorry, Trisha."

Her pulse kicked up a notch at his nearness.

How she had hoped against hope they could be a couple again. Now it appeared her dreams might come true.

"I regret my cowardly actions," Walker whispered, then squeezed her fingers and pulled her a little closer. She held a protective hand against his chest, as though maybe this apology would not be as easy as he thought.

Walker gazed into her brilliant green eyes, so full of life and love. How had he pushed away the woman he loved more than life itself? His heart thundered in his chest that God would give him a second chance at love. True love.

Before she'd arrived two months ago, he'd had a hard time trusting. He definitely hadn't believed he'd ever love again. But with God's help and life with Trisha, he could finally not only love again, but trust in that love.

"I don't think I can express how heartbroken I am for choosing fear over you." He drew her hand up and kissed her soft skin. Right then, he felt her relent a little. "I wouldn't blame you if you stayed mad at me, because I should never have broken things off in a panic.

Or made a decision like that without consulting God, but I was afraid."

Gently, she stepped an arm's length back and cocked her head. "What are you saying?"

"Pushing you away was a mistake, and I am so very sorry." His eyes pleaded with her. He hoped his remorse over the fear he'd felt showed through. "You are the best motherly influence for the children. The best comanager I could ever have for this barn. I got scared after your concussion." Regret knifed at him over the poor decisions he had made. "It felt like the car accident all over again and I freaked out. I couldn't protect you, and I did the only thing I could think of."

"You ran."

His face fell. "I did, and I promise I'll never do that again. Next time, and there probably will be a next time, I choose you over fear."

Her features relaxed, and he hoped she'd finally be able to put this past week, and all his blunders, behind them.

"Can you ever forgive me?"

She pulled his hand to her mouth and brushed her lips against his palm. "Of course I can."

His chest squeezed at those four simple, loving words. He wrapped his arms around her, cradling the back of her head and breathing her in.

"I love you and want to spend forever with you."

A slow, delightful smile crossed her face. She ran a finger along his scruffy jawline and he shivered. Boy, he'd missed her touch. She grounded him, made him feel alive.

"Don't you think we should go on a date before professing our undying love for each other?"

"Dating is overrated. But if you insist, there's a fancy restaurant not far from here…"

"I hear Eatalian Pizza makes an amazing lasagna. We could even share an antipasto."

He grinned. "Now you're talking my language. Tonight at, say, seven?" Excitement hummed around them.

"Let's make it six. We have three children who have a bedtime routine I'd prefer not to disrupt."

He tugged her close, leaned down and kissed her.

His heart hammered in his chest. They were back together again, stronger than before.

Now, with God at the helm, they were in it for the long haul.

"And a little more good news. Kent will be here for the meet and greet this weekend."

Her lips parted in surprise. "You're kidding me?"

"Nope. Looks like the kids get to grow up here after all."

"And I can be the barn manager," she said, contentment winding around her words and filling the air.

He gave her one last kiss before the crazy day took them by storm.

"What do you say we get back to the house so the kids don't become worried?" he whispered.

She threw her head back and laughed, taking his hand as they headed out of the barn. "As soon as I step foot in that kitchen, the girls are going to hijack me and insist on knowing everything that went on out here."

Then she slid him that sideways smile that made his pulse jump.

Thank You, God, for bringing Trisha into my life and letting me find true love once again.

Epilogue

Two months later, the leaves were changing color. A few had dropped, swirling every time someone strode over them. Trisha eyed her friend. "Why do you want to go to the pond now? I thought you wanted to ride Goliath?" she asked. It thrilled her the gelding had not only become a tame horse, but one that several riders now leased. He would win many blue ribbons next year at shows.

"I do," Autumn stated as she rounded the utility vehicle and stuck the key in the ignition. "But ever since Laney mentioned the sunsets opposite the pond, I thought it would be a perfect place for pictures at dusk." She clicked open a compact and lined her lips with a sparkly lip gloss.

As Trisha slid into the passenger seat, her phone dinged with an incoming text.

Clinic for October is full. Update the website, Kent texted.

Excited, she grabbed Autumn's arm and told her.

"It's so neat he offered to do a series of clinics for you guys," Autumn said, then refocused on her compact.

"He also offered to do another series next spring and summer."

"No kidding? What with Kent volunteering his services and Walker picking up some part-time work with his cybersecurity company, it seems like the fate of the horse farm is secure."

What a few months they'd had. Saving the farm, falling in love and both leaving their careers to work at the horse farm full-time.

"Yes, thanks be to God." What a journey it had been. They'd both learned a lot, including the living example of walking by faith, not sight. She glanced at her friend as Autumn closed the compact. "What do you want to get pictures of and for what?"

"Social media, silly."

"But you don't—"

"I'm committing to spend more time on it." Her voice was firm. "So, I need some good photos."

That didn't sound like Autumn at all, but it shouldn't take too long to snap a few pictures of her and still get a ride in before Cora returned with the children. Cora and Wade had invited all their grandchildren over for an afternoon of swimming, followed by a cookout. Trisha was touched they had included Sophie, Tommy and Gabby.

"I have an idea. Why don't we take some selfies?" Autumn said. "Here, let me put some gloss on your lips." She leaned over with the wand.

Trisha waved her friend off. "I'm fine."

"I want the pictures to be pretty and get lots of likes," Autumn said as she pouted. *Oh my.*

"Fine." She sat still while her friend applied the lip gloss, then pulled out a makeup pouch and added blush to her cheeks. When the mascara came out, Trisha put her hands up. "Enough, Autumn."

"Of course," she said, looking sheepish as she returned

the makeup to the bag and started the UTV. The farm that had once been unfamiliar was now second nature to not only Trisha and Walker, but the kids as well.

She'd been here four months. All three kids had started school a month ago and were adjusting well. They appreciated Friday movie night even more now that they were in school.

When the UTV came to the crest of the hill, the pond sat to the right. But the old gazebo caught her attention because Walker was standing at the entrance. Sophie, Tommy and Gabby stood in front of him, all dressed up.

Her heart flip-flopped at the sight of the man she loved with all her being.

"What's going on?" she asked.

Autumn didn't say a word, but grinned like she knew something.

Her friend pulled the vehicle to a stop off to the side and jutted her chin in Walker's direction. "Why don't you ask him?"

Trisha stood and brushed her damp palms against her new jeans, thankful Autumn had insisted on shopping earlier and encouraged her to wear her new clothes. Because if this was what she thought it was, she wanted to look special. She strode across the recently mowed field.

The gazebo held a gleaming coat of fresh white paint. Barely visible twinkle lights twined back and forth across the inside of the roof structure. The sun had just dipped behind the trees, creating the most enchanted lighting.

The paint, the twinkle lights, the mowed field: someone had put serious thought into this moment. Now she understood the shopping spree and the makeup Autumn had foisted on her. What a good friend.

Sophie bounced on her toes. An excited look covered

her face. Tommy appeared bored and shifted uncomfortably against his Sunday clothing. Gabby waved and grinned, looking adorable, wearing a matching outfit with her sister.

Trisha lifted her gaze to Walker. When had he found the time to shave and change into dress clothes? His Western shirt had pearl-snap fasteners and his dress boots looked sharp against his dark blue jeans. Without a cowboy hat on, his brown gentle waves blew in the breeze.

As the kids moved to the side, she stepped up to him. Excitement flitted in her belly.

"Glad you could make it," he said, his chocolate eyes twinkling with his words.

"I d-didn't," she stuttered, overwhelmed, and then touched a hand to her chest. "Autumn said—"

He reached for her hand. "I can take it from here."

That was one thing she loved about Walker. He took charge, but in the most loving way.

Keeping eye contact, Walker knelt on one knee.

Her heart thundered in her chest and she clasped her lips together in excitement.

"Sweetheart, I love you. To the moon and back." That was a quote from one of Sophie's favorite books, and Trisha adored that he'd used those sweet words at a time like this.

He took out a jewelry box and opened it. A gorgeous diamond ring sat nestled inside. Her heart leaped into her throat. She had never believed this would happen to her. God knew different.

"Trisha, will you marry me and the children?" His sweet words spiraled around her core like a hug. "We have this big hole that only you can fill and we need you."

The kids started clamoring, but Walker stood and gently hushed them.

"Yes, a hundred times yes." She threw her arms around his sturdy neck and breathed in his spicy scent.

When she leaned back, he moved his thumb on her cheek as he grazed her skin. Then he touched his lips to hers. She wrapped her arms around his shoulders.

Sophie cleared her throat and Trisha reluctantly pulled away. The love and forever she saw in Walker's gaze made her head swim.

"Can I see the ring?" Sophie asked as Trisha noticed movement in the background. Autumn with her swanky camera clicking away.

Trisha took off her college ring and tucked it in her pocket. She no longer needed the reminder of what she couldn't have because she'd be living her dream life before she knew it.

Walker slid the engagement ring on and she lifted her hand to appreciate the sparkle. That was why Sophie had wanted to do her nails last night. The seven-year-old had started by asking Trisha to do hers, hot pink. Then she'd asked if she could try to paint Trisha's. She'd done a gorgeous job, and the ring looked prettier with burgundy color on her nails.

Before she knew it, Autumn collected them all together and did a couple of staged shots. Then just the husband-and-wife-to-be looking adoringly into each other's eyes, which was super easy.

"Congratulations," Cora said as she stepped into view. Wade emerged from a utility vehicle. Ethan, Laney and their girls pulled up next to his father.

Cora tugged her into an energetic embrace. "I couldn't be happier to have you as my daughter-in-love," she whispered. "We've been praying for you since Walker was born."

Tears threatened, but Trisha held them back. She'd always dreamed of having parents like Cora and Wade, and now she would. "I'm thrilled to become a part of your family."

"You already are, sweetie. You already are."

Someone set off a confetti cannon and multicolored bits of paper floated from above.

One by one, everyone congratulated them. The women examined the ring and called it exquisite. Walker clung to her hand as though they were now inseparable. But Cora's words, *You already are*, wound around her heart along with her deep love for Walker.

The perfect man, the sweetest children, and the most loving and encouraging extended family she could ever hope for. Everything Trisha had always dreamed of but was convinced would never happen.

* * * * *

Dear Reader,

Thank you for joining me on this second journey to Serenity, Texas. Serenity Stables was inspired by the stable where I rode horses as a youngster. I have such happy memories of those carefree times.

For this romance, I chose two people skittish about relationships and completely afraid to trust. Throw in three cute orphans and what's not to love? Trisha learns that even though men may walk away from you, God never leaves His children. Walker's story revolves around how he blames himself for the unfortunate accident that took his wife. He discovers he must forgive himself before he can move on and live a new chapter in his life. Forgiveness is such a hard thing, but Walker learns that with God it can be beautiful.

I hope you enjoyed reading this story as much as I enjoyed writing it. It would be fantastic to connect with you. Drop me a note at heidimain.com. While there, you can sign up for my newsletter for book news, giveaways and life reports.

Hugs,
Heidi

COMING NEXT MONTH FROM
Love Inspired

AN AMISH MOTHER FOR HIS CHILD
Amish Country Matches • by Patricia Johns

After giving up on romance, Verna Kauffman thought a marriage of convenience would give her everything she's longed for—a family. But marrying reserved Adam Lantz comes with a list of rules Verna wasn't expecting. Can they overcome their differences to discover that all they really need is each other?

HER SCANDALOUS AMISH SECRET
by Jocelyn McClay

A life-changing event propels Lydia Troyer to return to her Amish community to repair her damaged reputation—with a baby in tow. And when she finds old love Jonah Lapp working on her family home, she knows winning back his trust will be hardest of all...especially once she reveals her secret.

FINDING THEIR WAY BACK
K-9 Companions • by Jenna Mindel

Twenty-eight years ago, Erica Laine and Ben Fisher were engaged to be married...until Erica broke his heart. Now, as they work together on a home that Erica needs to fulfill her new role as a traveling nurse, their past connection is rekindled. But can love take root when Erica is committed to leaving again?

FOR THE SAKE OF HER SONS
True North Springs • by Allie Pleiter

Following a tragedy, Willa Scottson doesn't hold much hope for healing while at Camp True North Springs. But swim instructor Bruce Lawrence is determined to help the grieving widow and her twin boys. This is his chance to make amends—if Willa will let him once the truth comes out...

THE GUARDIAN AGREEMENT
by Lorraine Beatty

When jilted bride Olivia Marshall is forced to work with her ex-fiancé, Ben Kincaid, it stirs up old pain. Yet she finds herself asking Ben for help when her four-year-old nephew is abandoned on her doorstep. Will their truce lead to a second chance...or will Ben's past stand in their way?

SAVING THE SINGLE DAD'S BOOKSTORE
by Nicole Lam

Inheriting his grandfather's bookstore forces Dominic Tang to return to his hometown faced with a big decision—keep it or sell. But manager Gianna Marchesi insists she can prove the business's worth. Then an accident leads to expensive damages, making Dominic choose between risking everything or following his heart...

LOOK FOR THESE AND OTHER LOVE INSPIRED BOOKS WHEREVER BOOKS ARE SOLD, INCLUDING MOST BOOKSTORES, SUPERMARKETS, DISCOUNT STORES AND DRUGSTORES.

LICNM1123

Get 3 FREE REWARDS!

We'll send you 2 FREE Books **plus** a FREE Mystery Gift.

FREE
Value Over
$20

Both the **Love Inspired®** and **Love Inspired® Suspense** series feature compelling novels filled with inspirational romance, faith, forgiveness and hope.

HARLEQUIN
PLUS

Try the best multimedia subscription service for romance readers like you!

Read, Watch and Play.

Experience the easiest way to get the romance content you crave.

Start your **FREE TRIAL** at
www.harlequinplus.com/freetrial.